SOMEONE SEEKING
SOMEONE ELSE

NICOLE FALLS

THANK YOU

TO FUNMI, ROSLYN, TAIMA: THANK YOU FOR YOUR COMPREHENSIVE FEEDBACK DURING THIS PROCESS

TO SHAKEIA: THANK YOU FOR YOUR CHECK-INS AND BEING MY FRIEND

TO THE WRITE CLUB: YOUR CONSISTENT ENCOURAGEMENT, THE SPRINTS, AND THE LAUGHS WERE ALL INSTRUMENTAL TO ME PRESSING FORWARD

TO COUSIN D: THANK YOU FOR YOUR KINDLE EXPERTISE (INSIDER) LOL

TO CHRISTINA: I ASKED YOU WHAT TO WRITE NEXT AND YOU TOLD ME THIS, SO HOPEFULLY YOU ENJOY LMAO

TO ANYONE ELSE I MAY HAVE FORGOTTEN, CHARGE IT TO MY HEAD AND NOT MY HEART, THIS ONE HAS BEEN A PROCESS. XO.

ONE

KAI

I made a mistake.

Those weren't four words that came out of my mouth often. Not that mistakes weren't ever made by me, *because they were*, but I just...didn't easily admit to them often. In this moment, however, as I sat across from a man who had not said anything to me for at least three minutes, but just peered at me with an unreadable expression etched across his features? I knew that I'd made a mistake. *Try the apps*, they said. *It would be a good way to judge just how serious you are about making this move*, they said. Well, I couldn't wait to tell them that they were wrong as hell. The apps did nothing to shore up my confidence that I was really ready to open my heart...*and legs* to someone new. I'd been single for so long. Comfortable in my singleness for so long that...maybe I was buggin'. Maybe it was a glitch in the matrix that woke me up one morning with a single-minded doggedness to find The One.

My life was perfect...*mostly*. I was the picture of perfect health, thanks to a very meticulous self-care routine, a fanatic relationship with the gym, and extremely iron-clad willpower. My relationships with my family and friends were awesome. I worked for myself, making a really good amount of money doing something that I loved beyond belief. I had zero room for complaint. To the outside world looking in, I was the epitome of goals on all levels...except one if you were into being partnered.

Which, typically was something that was neither here nor there for me. So I couldn't explain why, out of nowhere, I woke up about a month ago feeling like something was missing. And not a passing, fleeting feeling of "perhaps, maybe", but like a crater of cavernous depths had settled into the pit of my stomach, taking up permanent residence. I tried interrogating it on my own before bringing it up to my own personal tribunal council—made up of the four women on Earth who were closest to me and knew me better than myself. I'd approached each of them separately and the conclusion that they all came to was maybe I really did want to finally find the yin to my yang...be someone's rib.

And speaking of ribs, I looked around the restaurant to see where the hell our waiter was with the appetizer order that we'd put in what seemed like an eternity ago. I was on a date with a man I'd met on an internet dating site who was...not completely as advertised. Joe was fine as hell, so at least it wasn't catfish, but...it wasn't not catfish either. The charismatic, talkative man who kept my phone buzzing in the week since that we'd matched was nowhere to be seen. Instead in his place was a possible mute who answered my questions and attempts at making conversation with one to two words.

Taking a deep breath, I decided to try and break up the silence once again, "Is everything okay, Joe? Should we try to do this another time?"

"That... would probably be best," he replied, that one

sentence being the most words he'd strung together in succession all night.

"I...um...okay?" I replied as he immediately stood, tossed a few bills on the table and left wordlessly.

"What in the hell just happened?" I wondered aloud as the waiter finally returned with the heaping pile of fried deliciousness that made up the appetizer platter we'd settled upon ordering.

"Is... everything okay, miss?" the waiter asked, looking just as puzzled as I felt.

"Can you box this all up for me? And bring the check?"

"No problem, miss. Anything else I can get you?"

"That's all," I replied, shaking my head as I pulled out my cell phone to check the time before I sent a text.

Apps were all boxed, and the bill was paid. Joe ended up leaving me with a couple few extra coins than was necessary to cover the bill and tip. I pocketed that money as hazard pay then rocketed straight from the restaurant to the very comfortable chaise that was stationed in the woman cave of my dearest friend, Corin. She was the one I'd texted before I left the family friendly, casual dining restaurant to which Joe had invited me. A restaurant that gave me pause because both of us had previously expressed disdain for these types of restaurants pretty early on in our conversations, but I went along with the flow. Because apparently that's what this new "I'm desperate for steady, warm dick and maybe companionship as well" me was into. New Kai acquiesced without question. I...was starting not to like New Kai very much. As Old Kai I had been doing pretty well for myself. This new bitch got stood up for seemingly no good reason.

By the time I'd made it to Corin's house, her husband Wes and daughter Penelope were nowhere to be found. I'm sure they were just on the other side of this massive estate that they had the nerve to call a single-family home, but I was thankful to not have had to put on a façade of happiness in their presence. I had gone through all seven stages of grief in the fifteen-minute car ride from the restaurant to Corin's and was on my second cycle of them, currently stewing in the anger stage. One look at my face when she opened the door sent Corin into Super Best Friend mode—ushering me straight into the aforementioned woman cave, pouring a very large glass of my favorite sparkling wine, and remaining completely silent until I began speaking.

"Was this shit always this hard, Co? Is there something wrong with me? I used to be good at dating, when I did date back during the Carter administration, right? I'm a catch, right?"

"Unfortunately. Hell no. Hell yes. Undoubtedly," Corin answered, so quickly I'd forgotten what questions I'd asked in which order, "What happened, Kai? This was the guy you'd been telling me about. From the dating site? With the good vibes? And the *I give good dick* cut of his jib from photographs?"

I nodded, "Yeah, Joe. Who was completely different from the man in the texts, so unless this was an elaborate ruse of a catfish...I don't know what the hell happened? His reception when I'd arrived—a few minutes later than our agreed upon time, but there was an accident on Route 83 that derailed me a bit—*was* a little chilly. I'd texted to let him know about the accident, though, and he replied like everything was all good. So, I don't know what happened between that exchange and my eventual arrival that completely turned him off of me, but...yeah..."

"And are you going to try to follow up and see what happened or..." Corin started before I cut her off, "Abso-*the fuck*-lutely not! Whatever he has going on is of no concern to me."

Fully seated in my anger, I sat back taking a large sip of my wine before sighing.

"This whole thing is stupid. Nothing is wrong with my life as is, so why...oh my is my brain hellbent on trying to make me believe that something is lacking? I should be able to logic my way out of this. Go ahead...say something, I can see you're holding back," I prompted Corin.

She shook her head, "Nope. We're not there yet. We're still in the letting you get this exasperation off portion of this convo, chick."

I'd opened my mouth to go off yet again when my phone sounded off. I looked down to see it was Joe calling me.

"Oh, this motherfucker has got to be kidding me," I groused while sending him to voicemail, swiftly, "Now you got something to say? Fuck off."

I tossed my phone onto the table in front of my chaise and slammed my now empty glass down next to it. Corin got up and eased the glass away from me, murmuring under her breath about me having reached my limit on the wine. When the phone beeped again to indicate that Joe had indeed left a voicemail Corin looked at me, eyes communicating the question of whether or not I'd actually listen to the voicemail. I shook my head no.

"You know what the most messed up part of this is?" I asked.

Corin shook her head.

"The fact that I wasted a cheat day on this negro and he took me to fucking *Applebees. Applebees*, Co! When is the last time you willingly went to *Applebees*?"

"How many times are you gonna say *Applebees*, love? Never mind...to answer your question, never?" Corin replied, laughing.

"Okay, you don't sound too sure. But I'm certain your *born with a silver spoon in her mouth* behind probably has never even stepped foot in an *Applebees* period, but girl…I've tried to stay away from them since that short-lived stint of working there in undergrad. Anyway, that's not the point. The point is if you are a forty-three-year-old man taking a woman out on a first date, would you take her to *Applebees*? Probably not. Which should have been my first red flag, but I ignored it. Only to show up and this man is cosplaying a damn deaf mute. But still I persevered. Because…well, honestly, his fineness was a light at the end of the tunnel. I thought at the very least if I hadn't found the one, then I could at least get laid by the Dondre T. Whitfield looking brotha sharing table space with me, but he couldn't even get that right. And now he wanna call me? And think I'm gonna answer? Or even listen to a voicemail that is probably filled with lies and platitudes? For. Get. That. And him! And why did you take away my wine?"

"Are you sleeping here tonight?" Corin asked.

I nodded with a pitiful look on my face. I just didn't want to go home to another lonely night in bed. Corin sighed, then brought me a newly refilled glass of wine, along with a glass of water. I guzzled down half of the glass of bubbles before sighing contentedly and releasing a little burp.

"Are you staying down here or coming up to your room?" Corin asked.

"Down here, my blankie's still here, yeah?" I asked, stretching out on the chaise.

Corin didn't answer verbally, but instead retrieved the blanket that I'd brought back from a recent trip to Marrakesh from whatever hiding place the maid had stashed it and tossed it in my direction. I wrapped myself up in the blanket like a burrito, leaving one arm free to grab my wine glass once again.

"Are you really not gonna say anything, Co? About this

date? My expectations? Any of this shit show that is currently my life right now?"

Her lack of speaking was...disconcerting. Corin always had something to say, even when I didn't wanna hear it, which usually led to us going back and forth a bit. Tonight, I guess sis wasn't beat for the conversation or the arguing. She just gave me wine, let me rant, and then let me go.

Corin shook her head once again, "We'll talk about this in the morning. After Pen's game. Since you're here, you have to come. Don't try sneaking out before we get up, either. Because you know I'll sic her on you. And for the record, one bad date does not a shit show make."

I groaned, not only at her admonishing me like I was her child, but also at being roped into attending a darn soccer game in the morning. Corin, a former pro/Olympic level soccer player, coached her daughter's rec league team and took it a bit too seriously sometimes, much to mine, Wes, and Penelope's chagrin. Also, to the chagrin of the parents of children who I was sure signed their child up simply for the sake of getting them out of the house, not because they had any aspirations of their children being star athletes. Corin didn't believe in half-assing anything when it came to playing sports, and her intensity was welcomed since her family's name was on the building that housed the rec league.

Before completely disappearing up the stairs, Corin turned back to say something to me, "You know...I said I wasn't going to say anything, but I want to leave you with this. Have you ever thought that this yearning you're having to get back out there is less about coming from a place of lack, but more about just embellishing an already sweet existence? Think of it as whipped cream on a sundae. Is it necessary? Not really. Is it delicious as hell? Undoubtedly. Love you, Cobra...*do not* open another split of champers."

"Love you, too CoCo," I replied grumpily.

She had a point, but I was in belligerent mode, not trying to hear a thing adjacent to logic.

Against Corin's advice last night, I did open another split of Laurent-Perrier and currently found myself nursing a headache while trying to keep up with Penelope zooming down the soccer pitch like she was playing for the *Gold Stars*, our local semi-pro women's club. Corin was on the sidelines, yelling out commands to the entire team like a mad woman while Pen calmly directed the girls on the field. For an eleven-year-old, she held a remarkable amount of poise, which was surprising considering her highly excitable parents. To further prove my point, Wes jumped up, screaming, "That's my baby girl!" when Pen scored a goal shortly after my observation. He hadn't said much to me this morning, which was also surprising. Wes and I had a brother/sister like relationship, usually full of antagonistic teasing. Co must've warned him I was feeling a little worse for the wear, so he was pulled back.

To no great surprise, the team coached by Corin won, trouncing the other team so badly that the ref enacted the slaughter rule for most of the second half of play. Our team couldn't score any goals when they had possession of the ball until the opposition scored one. The only problem with that? Our girls were too good on defense to allow them to score, so I rested my eyes for most of the second half, trying to reserve some energy to be as excited as I knew Pen would be once we were on our way to breakfast. As I sat in the backseat listening to Pen prattle on about "megging" some kid and feeling bad because he looked like he was about to cry, the FaceTime tone sounded off on my phone. I pulled it out of my bag to see my mother's name splayed across the screen, so I immediately swiped to answer.

"Hey, ma!"

"Hey baby…where are you?"

"Came out with Co, Wes, and Pen to Pen's game...I just rode with them to make things simpler. Say hey to everyone, they can hear you..."

They all exchanged pleasantries before I dug out my AirPods and placed them in my ears. Mama claimed she was calling me to check up since I'd apparently called her in the middle of the night crying about not being good enough to get and keep a man. *Jesus God I was on one last night!* I thought, while verbally reassuring her that everything was all good. I must've really been deep in the well of my feelings though because my mother was currently in Italy on her eat pray love shit with my auntie/godmother Didi. Our conversation was short because I didn't want to delve too far into everything that occurred last night in mixed company, but my mother made me promise to call her and Aunt Didi back the minute I got home.

"Goddy?" Penelope called out.

"Yeah, babe?" I replied.

"Are you sleeping over again tonight? We haven't had a sleepover in a while. You've been gone for like...*forever*."

I shook my head, "Not tonight, babe. Last night's sleepover was an accident, but we'll plan something soon. I should be in town for quite some time now," I said.

Pen sighed, "You said that last time though and then you were in Africa for *forever*..."

"Is forever our new favorite word?" I asked, meeting Corin's eyes in the side view mirror as she tried muffling her laughter, "I was only gone for three weeks, babe. Hardly forever. But how about we set a date now, so it's on my calendar. Since you don't trust me..." I trailed off.

"You're so dramatic, Goddy. It's not that I don't trust you, it's just that you stay too busy," Penelope said shaking her head and holding her hand out for my phone.

I gladly handed it over, letting her navigate to the

calendar app to find some free time to schedule our grossly overdue Goddy and Pen time. I took being her godmother very seriously and was just about completely bowled over when Corin and Wes approached me before her christening asking if I would be Penelope's godmother. Co was the first of my friends to settle and have kids, so I had no idea what exactly being a godmother entailed, but I was down with it. Growing up I'd been close with my own godmother, but she was also my mother's sister, so I felt like I would have naturally had that kinship with my aunt anyway. I modeled Pen and mine's relationship after the template of mine and Aunt Didi's, and if Penelope's complaining about not seeing me often enough was any indication? It seemed like I was knocking this godmother thing out of the park.

"Here you go," Penelope said, handing my phone back.

"Wait…"I said, looking at the calendar app that she'd left open, "You booked a whole weekend?"

She nodded, grinning broadly, "We've got a lot to catch up on."

After breakfast, I left the Moores to their business and went home to put in a few hours of work—the one downside to working for yourself. I didn't really have any traditional days off, though I'd given up running the day to day of my website. What had begun as a joke URL more than ten years ago had grown into a lifestyle website wherein, I used my undergraduate psychology major skills to uplift and encourage women to control their own destiny by charting a path that led to them following their hearts and minds. *TheresMoreToLifeThanDick.com* was started on a dare from Corin and neither of us had any idea that it would take off as quickly as it had.

My undergraduate roommate was going through a devastating breakup and the website had started as a blog that was initially a series of letters reminding her of her worth and the many things of value she had to add to the world beyond being her ex's girl. The posts went from being passed around in our friend circles, to gaining a following on Facebook, then Twitter when it emerged as a space for bloggers to flourish. I went from publishing once or twice a week to maintaining a schedule of posts on a variety of subjects, curating workshops and meet-ups based on the founding principles of the site and growing an almost cult-like following before stepping back to let my team of managing editors handle the majority of the workload a couple of years ago.

Now that I was more of a figurehead, my presence in the offices of *More to Life...* was infrequent as I had a capable staff that I trusted to run things smoothly. I was very much present in the decision making for directions in which we were looking to travel, but the day-to-day minutiae was handled by my staff. As I sat going through my inbox, I wondered if this were part of the problem. I had a massive social media presence and rarely logged off. Even if I wasn't actively doing anything, I spent my downtime scrolling through the internet aimlessly, clicking hither and thither to pass the time. Maybe I just needed to unplug completely, instead of the normal monthly seventy-two hour fast I had as a part of my routine now.

The man of my dreams probably didn't even know what the internet was...some rugged mountain man type who worked the land he owned with his bare hands, barely receiving telephone or television signals wherever he lived, getting his news the old fashioned way—via newspaper or telegram or the pony express or something. I could imagine him in my mind vividly, after a long day of working his land he would settle in next to the fire with a newspaper—reading it from cover to cover. He probably spent his evenings lamenting the fact that he had yet to find me, *his perfect Mrs.*

Right, as he scanned the paper, wondering where she was. But—what if I went analog, straight up old school and placed an ad right in the paper, then he saw it? We'd connect instantly and live happily ever after. Giggling, I shook off my flights of fancy and kept moving through my inbox, clearing as much of it that I could without bothering any of my staff on their days off. Anything that wasn't easily solved, I filed away for the Monday morning meeting.

For the rest of the night though, that idea of placing the personal ad kept niggling at me. Instead of paying attention to the Law & Order SVU marathon about unlawful clergymen and women, I was googling how to construct a personal ad for a newspaper. For kicks and giggles, I put one together for myself before turning my attention back to Benson and Stabler. But the thought of placing the ad kept niggling at me, so I shot off a quick text to my cousin Tina.

Hey, T. Is it too late to get a personal ad in the paper before it's put to bed?

Despite the fact that she was only an admin in the office of our local newspaper, *The Belleview Gazette*, Tina did almost everything in that darn office. So, I knew if there was a way to get it in there tonight, she'd find it. No sooner than I'd sent that text, my phone rang. I answered it without looking.

"Hello?"

"Please don't tell me this is a stunt for *More to Life*, Kai. I can't ask for this favor if it is," Tina said in lieu of a greeting.

"No, it's not a stunt, Tee. I promise," I replied, sounding anxious to my own ears.

"You can't just use the apps like the rest of us, Kai? You always gotta be extra," Tina laughed.

"Listen, I tried the apps like y'all told me to, cuzzo and I ended up with an inbox full of men who were nothing like what I'd clearly stated that I wanted in my profile. And when I finally found one who seemed to be about something? He turned out to be a serious dud. Like left me in the *Applebee's* on Route 83 type dud," I whined.

"Wait…little miss bougie went to an *Applebee's*? Was there documentation of this? I don't believe you, you need more people. Also…dude, don't you know the number one rule of dating apps is dudes don't read? This is why you have to pick through the weeds to find the flowers and initiate contact, cuz. Dang, have I taught you nothing?" Tina giggled.

"Apparently not! Why didn't you put me up on this game when I was talking to you and CoCo about this all of those weeks ago in the group chat?"

"I'm fronting big time, Kai. My scary behind barely sends a man a 'hello', but from what I hear…" Tina started.

"Save your hearsay, I've had enough of that. Look, can you get the ad in the paper tonight or nah? Coz if so, I've been googling and I…"

"You really went and googled personal ads?" Tina giggled again.

"It's a slow Sunday, Tee. And stop making fun of me!"

Still laughing Tina continued, "Okay, but you do know that the average age of our subscribers is a solid fifty-four, so like…are you looking for a sugar daddy or…well, thinking about the financial demographics of our readership he'd be more like a Splenda sweetie, but…"

"Celestine No Middle Name Because Ya Mama Didn't Love You Clay, two things—why do you know all of that demographic info and most importantly, can you help me or not?"

"Well," Tina harrumphed, "with that kind of energy…"

"Pleeeease, Tee. I will owe you forever and however you want."

I didn't know why I was so desperate for her to get this done tonight, but at some point in my mind this seemed like less of a lark and more of a solid idea. And if all else failed, I'd definitely turn it into an editorial in the *Kai's Korner* section of *More to Life*...even though I'd told Tina this wasn't a stunt for the website. Which, *it truly was not*, but if it backfired, I would be a fool not to use it.

"Text me your copy and I'll see what I can do," Tina agreed.

"See, that's why you're my favorite cousin! You always got my back."

"I'm your only cousin, fool!"

"Semantics, Tee," I laughed, "Semantics. Seriously though, if you pull this out tonight you'll be the real MVP. I will owe you big time!"

"Even bigger than when I got in trouble for running that ad for *More to Life* a few years ago? I still haven't lived down your usage of the eggplant emoji and the hubbub it raised amongst our subscribers."

"Ok, but in my defense..." I trailed off.

"You have none," Tina finished, knowing my trademark phrase.

"See...that's what I mean, Tee. You always got my back!"

"Mmmmhmmm, now when I cash in on all these favors, in the near future don't be surprised," Tina chuckled.

"Whatever you want, it's yours, sister-cousin!"

"Yeah yeah, I'll hit you back later if I'm able to make this happen. I'm running low on favors from Jacques."

"Aye, make sure that fine, creole motherfucker knows this is my ad because he could definitely get an audition for the spot of number one bae, okay?"

Jacques was the editor of the *Gazette*, a kid we went to high school with who up and got fine while off in college. Brother went from geek to chic and never looked back.

"Trust me, you don't want them problems," Tina grumbled, "More Vienna sausage than Andouille..."

I gasped before breaking out into laughter, "Tee, you hit that?"

"Girl, he is so flirty that I had to—*for the culture*. And that one time was enough. Tina did that so Kai don't have to go through that," Tina laughed, "But for real, lemme get off this phone and call him to see if we can get this in there. I'll hit you back later."

"Thanks, TinaBina! Love you, talk to you later."

I went back to watching Law & Order until I received a text from Tina thirty minutes later saying that the deed had been done and I immediately went into freak-out mode. This was a major mistake. I should have just stayed with the booty call apps like the rest of the single aunties and saw what was poppin'. This ad was about to bring all the toothless grandpas who read the paper daily to the yard and none of the fine, age-appropriate professionals that I desired. My return text to Tina tried to get her to get it rolled back, but it was too little too late. She'd already had to commit to going out with Jacques again to get him to bend the rules and wasn't about to recant because I had second thoughts. My impulsive nature had caught up with me once again, writing a check that I wasn't sure my ass was ready to cash.

TWO

RUX

"I ain't got nothing but time, peanut. We can do this all day if you want to," I said, trying not to chuckle at the pout that covered the face of the five-year-old with whom I was currently engaged in an epic stare off, "You don't scare me. And what I do know is that you are gonna find some space in your tummy for at least two more pieces of broccoli or dessert is cancelled."

"One more?" Harlow attempted to bargain.

"Two. Take it or leave it," I replied, as firmly as I could without breaking character.

Harlow's mother had way more practice at playing bad cop than I had, but I was a quick study. Since she'd been spending more and more time at my place, I'd had to go back and forth between being Fun Dad, the respite from Mean Mama and a staunch disciplinarian—which was markedly less fun. LowLow was a pretty chill kid, most often our clashes happened when she didn't want to eat her veggies with dinner. Since she had only been with me three nights a week and every other weekend for the past nine months, she didn't really take me super seriously when I tried on the bad cop role. That didn't stop me from persevering, even when she pinned me with that wide-eyed gaze starring those big brown eyes that mirrored my own. I held up two fingers and wriggled them in front of her. Harlow sighed before slumping backwards in her chair.

"Welp," I said, moving from where I sat across from her at the table toward the refrigerator, "Guess I'll have to enjoy this cookies and cream ice cream by myself."

As I pulled the hand packed pint out of the freezer, opened it and stuck a spoon in to take a bite Harlow's eyes grew even wider. I walked back over to where she sat – *not eating* – to rub it in a bit more.

"Daddy! We were supposed to share!" she gasped.

"And you," I said, booping her on the nose, "were supposed to keep your end of the bargain and eat everything on your plate. What happened to being Captain of the Clean Plate Club, huh?"

"I don't wanna be a captain. I wanna eat ice cream," Harlow whined, poking out her lower lip.

"It's two itty bitty pieces of broccoli, kid. That's all that stands between you and this sweet, creamy delight," I said, scooping another large bite into my mouth and humming with delight as I walked away from the table.

"Is it really delicious, daddy?" Harlow asked, mouth damn near watering as she watched the movement of my spoon digging into the soft ice cream once again.

"Mmmhmm," I said, exaggerating the flavor, "Might be the best ice cream I've had ever."

"Ever?" she parroted in an awe-struck tone.

"Ever." I said, sticking another spoonful into my mouth.

That one word spurred her into action. Harlow polished off those two pieces of broccoli on her plate in two seconds flat, hopping out of her chair at the table and running up to where I stood leaning against the counter eating the ice cream. I grabbed another spoon from the drawer before walking back toward the table so we could sit and eat from the pint together.

"You're right, daddy, this is the best ice cream ever!" Harlow mused, melted evidence of her enjoyment of the dessert all around her mouth.

Every time she called me daddy; it sent a jolt through my system. It was still so new that I was still trying to wrap my head around the fact that I was somebody's whole daddy outchea. A privilege I was almost completely robbed of thanks to the selfishness of Harlow's mother. She and I...had an agreement. One that was going pretty well until she'd abruptly ended it. For years I had no idea what had caused her sudden about face until I literally ran into Britt and Harlow coming out of the grocery store. I took one look at baby girl and those eyes and instantly knew that Britt had a lot of explaining to do. These past few months hadn't been the easiest, but we were slowly but surely working toward getting things on the right track.

"All right, Low, three more spoonsful and then it's bath and story time," I said, placing the pint of ice cream directly in Harlow's path.

I had to bite back even more laughter as she tried making those last three spoonsful count, piling as much ice cream on the spoon as she could before savoring those final bites. When Harlow finished, I put the ice cream back in the freezer and we headed upstairs to get our bath time routine completed. By the time we'd made it to story time, Harlow barely lasted through half of the book we were reading, *Black Girl Shine*, a children's book aimed at encouraging kids to be confident in all of the things they bring to the table in this world. It was one of Harlow's favorites, one we'd been reading repeatedly for the past three weeks. I'd have to tell my cousin's wife, who sent this book with a host of others for Harlow, that she had a hit on her hands with this one.

Since Harlow was finally down, it was now time for me to get to work. I had a pretty large order that I'd expected to finish before Britt dropped her off, but you know what they said about the best made plans. This new career path plus Harlow's appearance in my life had made for quite the eventful last year of my life. If anyone had said to me two years ago that not only would I no longer be a high-powered attorney, but that I would be also be parenting half-time while running my own custom greeting card business out of my house? I would have told them to get the fuck outta here. But here I was...in the midst of a life very different from the one I had envisioned for myself, but also one that I wouldn't trade for anything in the world. Thanks to a few well-placed advertisements and interviews, business was boomin' and only getting better. Pretty soon I'd have enough on my plate that I would have to hire some part-time help. I'd already put some feelers out at the local university's art department to make that vision a reality.

The project I was working on tonight was for a wedding —handmade place cards and menus. A night full of calligraphy was in my future with less than half of the order needing to be completed before I placed my head to the pillow tonight. I cranked up a Spotify Daily Mix session in my AirPods before getting down to business. Once I got in the zone, I ended up knocking out the rest of the wedding order and starting a couple of custom illustrations for a kid's party invitations. I sketched out the outline for the prototype of the invitation, but felt my eyes growing heavy so I decided to shut it down for the night. Even nine months in I wasn't completely adjusted to the energy that Harlow required me to keep up. We'd been out running all day since she was out of school and I had some things to take care of at my rental property. I had some time before I'd promised the party invitation proofs to my customer, so there was no use in me staying awake trying to sketch through sleepiness. I'd get back at it in the morning after Low went to school.

Morning found Harlow in a really chill mood, which made life much easier for me. We had a breakfast of my infamous waffles that she just couldn't get enough of, sausage, and eggs.

"Daddy, you always make the bestest waffles!" Harlow declared as she chewed one of the aforementioned waffles.

"Chew, then speak peanut," I immediately replied, chuckling to myself at how easily I slipped into Dad Mode.

She was too busy having the time of her life with her breakfast to pay me any never mind, as she drizzled a bit more syrup onto her entire plate. Watching her pick up the sausage patty with her fingers and slide it through the river of syrup that currently ran all around her plate before popping it into her mouth, I smiled. *Definitely my kid* I thought. We both had the same insane sweet tooth, one that could never be satiated. Britt complained that I gave in too much when it came to Harlow having sugar, but she just assumed. She didn't know how things went down over here...*her choice*. Initially when I'd started visitation with Harlow, a court appointed guardian accompanied her until she got more comfortable with me and then her companion went away. I was still more than tight with Britt for keeping my baby girl away from me for so long, but I tried not to let that annoyance show during the times when Britt and I did have to interact. Couldn't say the same for her, but it was cool, though. Not even her mama's stank attitude could keep me and my baby apart.

"Alright kiddo, are you about done there?" I said, flicking up my wrist to check the time, "It's almost time for us to ride out to the schoolhouse."

"Daddy, school is not a house...it's...a school!" Harlow corrected me, giggling.

"Go wipe your face and wash those hands. And where's your backpack?"

Harlow took off running to do as I asked and didn't answer my question. I couldn't remember if she or I brought in her things last night, so I really had no idea where her backpack was. She was still in pre-k, having just turned five recently so the backpack was more for show and storage of her random art she brought home, but her mother would throw a conniption fit if she returned without that Doc McStuffins backpack. I went into the living room and saw it was on the couch, much to my relief. *One less thing to get into it with Britt about,* I thought. Harlow reappeared and I got her into her jacket before we hustled out of the house and into my warm, waiting car. Dropping her off at school with big kisses and a promise to find us an adventure to get into for next weekend, I headed back home to get back to work.

No sooner than I'd sat down at my drafting table, my phone went off, signaling an incoming FaceTime. I looked at the screen to see it was my cousin Wes, so I grabbed it swiping to connect with an easy smile on my face.

"Well well well, if it ain't the real househusband of Belleview. Whassup, bro?" I laughed when we connected.

"Oh, the *Belleview Gazette* cover boy got jokes, huh?" he laughed back.

"Cover boy?" I asked.

A few weeks ago, one of our former classmates who now wrote human interest articles for our hometown paper reached out to me when she got wind of my business and wanted to write up a little "hometown boy done good" type of article on the business and strong connections to our hometown. As someone who fully believed that all publicity was good publicity, I was eager to do it, sitting down with

Rachel and her photographer Andy when they drove out the couple hours to come see me for the interview. Harlow was with me when they came to visit, so Andy had snapped a few photos of us together, one of which Rachel was certain she'd be including in the write-up. Rachel had been in touch over the past week, letting me know that the article was to be published within the next few days, but she hadn't said anything about me being on the cover.

"Yep, look at you and little LowLow on the cover, my boy!" Wes crowed, flipping his camera so I could see the paper laid out flat on the table in front of him.

Below the fold, but not too shabby. The main picture in the article, cornily titled *It Was All in the Cards*, was a photo of me standing over Harlow's shoulders looking straight into camera as she stood on a step stool, chin in her hands, peering at an in-progress drawing on my drafting table. Objectively, it was a wild cute shot of me and my kid.

"Say bruh, send me a few copies?" I asked Wes, thinking that I wanted one to frame as well as to give to Britt and her parents.

"Already ahead of you, bro. Corin bought a whole stack to give to everyone we know. She put about ten in the mail for you to disperse as you see fit, too," Wes laughed.

"Sis always looking out. Where is she, so I can thank her?" I asked.

"In the gym...hold on, lemme go over there," Wes replied.

"Damn, must be nice to have everything you desire in arms reach, bruh. Do y'all ever leave the palatial estate?" I joked.

"Only when we throw bread at the peasants who live beyond our walls," Wes replied sarcastically.

Wes had married into *money* money, but his wife Corin, despite being raised with a platinum spoon in her mouth, was the most laid back, down to earth woman you'd ever meet. You would think that being absurdly rich along with a celebrity in her own right due to her status as a former Olympian would have her with her ass on her shoulders, but she was still the same gap-toothed Rinny who was a master at talking shit with the best of them back in high school. I still didn't know what she saw in Wes' big-headed ass, but they'd been going strong since we were like fourteen years old and showed no signs of slowing down. If I was the type of guy to buy into that relationship goals kind of shit, their relationship would definitely be the one I modeled any that I tried to pursue after. Well, the second relationship I'd model after, anyway. The first would be my aunt and uncle's, Wes' parents, who'd raised me like I was their own after my mom's death when I was four.

I didn't remember much of my life before coming to live with them, but I definitely had fond memories of life growing up with my brother-like cousin and the damn near perfect role models we'd had in both my aunt and uncle growing up. Aunt Lane was my mom's sister who looked damn near like her twin, which was a lot for me to bear when I'd initially moved in with them, but her and Uncle Weston both exhibited hella patience with me as I adapted to living with them. I'd never known anything about my dad, so Uncle Weston was the closest thing I had to one. Growing up the way I did made was what made me so upset with Britt when I first found out about Harlow, honestly. Despite she and I not being made for riding off into the sunset on some happily ever after jazz, she had no right to keep me away from my daughter—robbing me of even making the decision. I shook my head, ridding myself of those thoughts and tuned back into what Wes was talking.

He was just recapping his daughter's latest game, which, honestly if I'd seen one I'd seen them all. But I knew how that proud dad thing went and would gladly talk anyone's ears off for hours about Harlow, so I put on a pleasant expression, offering wordless interjections that seemed like I'd been completely tuned in all along.

"Anyway," Wes said, walking into their home gym, "Baby...The wants to talk to you."

"Aye man, I told you about that The shit. I ain't a Huxtable," I joked.

"Bruh, I ain't calling a grown man, Teddy. And I damn sure ain't calling you Rux. I don't feel comfortable, dawg. I been calling your ass The since we were kids, ain't no college rebrand changing that," Wes replied back.

"So, you're okay with calling me an article of speech, but not by my preferred name, got it!" I laughed.

"Man listen, I just started being able to keep up with the pronoun thang with some of these kids at Penny's school. My brain only got so much space for other shit now, The!"

"Man, where is Corin?" I laughed again at his silly ass.

"Hurry up, baby...this *my name is my name ass mofo* Theodore is thirsty to talk to you," Wes said, handing the phone over to Corin.

I just shook my head.

"Hey, RinnyRin. Good looks on the papers," I said, grinning when I saw her flushed face that indicated that she'd just finished a pretty strenuous workout.

"Why didn't you tell us you were gonna be on the front page, superstar!" Corin gushed.

"I had no idea, man. Rach ain't said a word about that in all these damn emails she's sent me in the past forty-eight hours," I laughed.

"She was probably just trying to impress you anyway. You know she still has that crush on you from high school. Every time I see her down at the grocery, she's asking about you," Corin teased.

"Chill out, Rin," I replied, shaking my head, "That girl

doesn't want me. She was a consummate professional when they came down here."

"Mmmhmm," Corin replied, like she knew something I didn't know.

I didn't even bother protesting more because I knew that it was pointless. Once Corin got her brain wrapped around something being a certain way, there was little to no room to change her mind.

"Aight, well I ain't gon hold you up, I know you just got done getting ya sweatin' to the oldies on, but I wanted to thank you for sending the papers...and the care package you sent Low a few weeks back. We've been reading that *Black Girl Shine* book nightly ever since."

"That's what's up. I'll have to let Pen know. She was the one who found that one on Instagram. And you don't have to thank me for any of that, brother. You know I got you. Also, you might wanna flip through the whole *Gazette* when you get it. Might be a few things inside that'll pique your interest," Corin grinned.

"Like what?" I asked, feeling like she wanted to say something but didn't want to say it directly.

"Oh...just new developments around town and such. Lots of fun stuff happening in The View that you might wanna catch up with," she replied coyly.

"Why does this feel like a set up?" I asked, laughing.

"It isn't! I'm just saying, you ain't that far from the crib, but you're far enough to be missing out on key developments in the area. It wouldn't hurt to keep abreast of the goings on of your hometown. That's all I'm saying..."

"Sure, Rin. Aight, for real. I'ma let y'all go. Tell your uglass husband I'll call him back later, I gotta get some work done. Love y'all."

"Love you too, Teddy. Oh! Don't forget Pen wants you to

design her birthday invites," Corin threw in before I could disconnect the call.

"I haven't forgotten at all, tell her to hit me up after she gets outta school so she can tell me the *vibe*," I replied.

Corin laughed at the inflection I put on for the word "vibe" since that was Pen's new thing. Everything was a vibe, needed to be a vibe, was the wrong vibe...she was killing me already and she wasn't even a teen, just about to turn twelve. Wes and Rin would have a ton of trouble on their hands as that girl continued to mature for damn sure. I hung up, tossed my phone aside, cranked some music in my AirPods, and got back to work on the sketches I'd abandoned last night. Pulling up the photos that my client had sent over for reference, I set about infusing the more intricate details of the faces I'd be drawing.

This was the part of my job that I liked the most honestly, recreating photos in my own unique drawing style was a special challenge in and of itself. Ensuring that I paid close attention to features, facial structures, and unique identifying bits of people and managing not to make it look like a caricature could sometimes prove to be difficult. Luckily, since I'd mostly converted to digital for work, erasing and starting over until I got it just right was a helluva lot easier. Definitely saved me a lot of paper, for damn sure.

I was in the middle of *swee-dee-do-do-dee-doop-deedeeing* right along with Donell Jones about where he wanted to be when my music was interrupted by an incoming voice call. Glancing at my phone's screen to see who was calling immediately made me roll my eyes when Britt's name flashed. *What the hell does she want?* I thought while swiping to answer the call.

"What's good, Britton?" I said, somewhat jovially since I was working on keeping the peace between us.

"I need you to take Harlow this weekend and I'll keep her next week on your weekend," she said, without a greeting.

"Oh, I'm doing well, thanks for asking," I replied, unable to keep the sarcasm out of my tone.

"Oh please, Rux. Let's not even start this shit today," she replied, "Can you keep her yes or no?"

"Of course, my daughter is always welcomed over here. When are you dropping her off?" I asked.

"See...that's the thing. I kinda need you to pick her up tonight from school and keep her through Tuesday. I would have just asked my mom, but she and my dad are still down south visiting family," Britton said, almost sounding annoyed that she had to explain herself.

"When you say through Tuesday, you mean like I can drop her back off to you Tuesday night or I should be making sure to drop her off for school on Wednesday?" I asked, just to be super clear.

She and I had these sorts of interpretation mix ups before and the last thing I needed was her ass being irritated with me once again because she wasn't clear.

"You can take her to school Wednesday, and I'll pick her up," Britt replied, tersely.

"Aight. Anything else I need to know? I know we have ballet tonight, but other than that?"

"Nope. I'll drop her ballet bag off by your place before you leave to get her from school."

"Aight, Britt. We good then?"

"Yep."

"Bet, talk to you later," I said, about to hang up.

"Rux! Wait," Britt called out before I could press the red button to hang up, "Thanks...for being so accommodating."

Britton sounded like she would rather have a root canal than actually thank me, but I let it go with a smooth you're welcome and disconnected the call. Having lil mama underfoot for the next few days definitely meant that I needed to stick to a real work schedule instead of the haphazard shit I usually defaulted to when it was just me. It also meant that adventure I promised earlier this morning would have to happen this weekend instead of the next. If the weather were warmer, I would have many more options, but since we were still experiencing a bit of a cold snap, I had no idea what we'd get into. She'd been hinting at wanting to go to the aquarium, so maybe I could turn that into something. In the meantime, I needed to get my ass out of the house because my cabinets and fridge were looking a little too light for my pint sized yet grown man appetite sized youngster to have an extended stay. I needed to make a grocery store run and come back to the house to put everything away before I had to pick her up.

[***]

"Daddy I'm bored, I thought you said we were going on an adventure today," Harlow whined, walking into my office and resting her head against my side.

"We are baby girl. Daddy's just gotta finish one itty bitty teeny tiny thing for work then we can hit the road, okay?" I replied as I straightened up from being hunched over on my desk and pressed a quick kiss to the top of her head, "It shouldn't take me any longer than one more episode of *True and the Rainbow Kingdom*, okay baby?"

"Okayyyyy," Harlow said as she slumped onto the couch in my office with her tablet.

I had all intention of us leaving out directly after breakfast so we could begin our day of fun, but an urgent email from a client stopped my stride. I needed to send her the updates she requested for her file revisions before I headed out for the day. I could have just let it linger until the evening since it was technically the client's fault that the images were incorrect, but I didn't run my business like that. If I was able to shift a few things to ensure the client's satisfaction was always paramount, then I did what I had to do to get things handled. Unfortunately, for Harlow customer satisfaction wasn't top of mind. So, I was pretty sure I'd be paying for the delay to her day of fun on the backend - outta my pockets.

Soon, I was finished with my work and we were out the door to the aquarium, our first stop on the day of fun. After the aquarium, we took a trip to the children's museum which, despite having been there at least a billion times before, was Harlow's favorite place to visit in our little city. Hours of meticulous perusal of exhibits she'd seen and played with countless times before, she still greeted with the same level of exuberance as if it was her first time coming into the place. Her energy was contagious as I found myself getting just as caught up in everything as she was. After the museum we grabbed lunch at her favorite restaurant and of course had a scoop of ice cream for dessert to accompany our meal. By the time we were traveling back home, baby girl was zonked—mouth open, snoring lightly with her head thrown back on the top of her car seat that she was damn near too big for. I made a mental note to look into either getting a larger one or moving her into just the booster seat that looked less like a car seat.

I knew that waking Harlow up to walk in the house was a no go, so I didn't even bother once I pulled into my driveway. I just hitched her over one shoulder and made my way toward the house. I noticed a large box waiting outside of my door but had no idea what the heck it was because I didn't remember ordering anything from Amazon recently. When I got to the door, I read the name on the return address and realized that this was the box that Corin sent with the copies of the paper in it. I could have sworn that she'd only sent a few though, so I didn't know why this damn box was so big. I unlocked the door with my keyless entry app before I bent down to scoop the box up with my free arm that wasn't cradling Low. It was a little bit heavier than I anticipated and I almost toppled my big ass over and dropped Harlow in the process trying to balance. My shifting around woke her up just as I crossed the threshold of the house and dropped the box inside.

"What's in the box, Daddy?" she asked, rubbing her eyes and yawning as I sat her down on the couch then put the box on the table in front of us so I could investigate its contents.

"Something from Auntie Corin, we gotta open it and see," I replied, pulling my keys out to use my little utility knife to pierce the tape sealing the box closed.

Those words made Harlow perk right on up, "Something for me?"

"I dunno, peanut. I thought it was just for me, but who knows?" I pulled back the flaps to see what the heck was in this box.

I laughed as I pulled out at least twenty-five copies of the *Belleview Gazette*. Wes wasn't lying when he said Rin bought out the store with the papers. I had no clue what she thought I was going to do with all these damned papers.

"It's me, daddy! I see me! And you!" Harlow exclaimed, scooching into my lap so she could get a closer view of the paper.

The picture of us looked even more adorable in person and I couldn't help grinning broadly as I replied to her, "It sure is, peanut!"

"Are we famous?" Harlow asked, awe covering her words.

"What do you know about famous, lil bit?" I asked, laughing.

"Well, I asked mommy why come it's always the same people on magazines when we we're at the grocery store and she said it's because they're famous cella babies," Harlow replied.

"Celebrities, baby," I correctly, gently.

"That's what I said. So, since we on the front of this paper, we cella babies, right daddy? I can't wait to take this to show and tell, so everybody can see me and my famous daddy," Harlow mused, mind completely made up that she and I were now "cella babies".

"If you say so, peanut," I laughed.

"I just did say so, daddy. You're silly," Harlow giggled as she settled back with her own copy of the paper to stare at our picture and pretend to read.

I grabbed another copy, reading the cover story before flipping through to about midway through the paper to read the rest of it. I'd have to send Rachel an *Edible Arrangement* for this joint because she made me sound doper than I knew I already was. I had no idea of the *Gazette's* true range, but maybe I'd pick up some business from this. It was cooler to me, though, to see myself on the front page of my hometown newspaper. *Mama I made it*, I joked to myself, chuckling soundlessly. I decided to flip through the *Gazette* and see if they still printed the police blotter near the back, right before the sports section.

On Saturday mornings, I remembered Aunt Lane reading the blotter out loud to Uncle Weston, clucking if she came across the name of someone she knew or recognized an address in one of the little blurbs with the petty crimes that were listed. Wes and I would pretend like we weren't really paying attention as she read, but our little ears were always perked up waiting to hear names we recognized as well as she went through. Hell, he and I almost ended up in the damn blotter ourselves one time, when he got the grand idea to spray paint his undying love and adoration for Corin in the massive driveway of her family's estate. Luckily, the

Bellegraves decided not to press charges when we were caught by their security trying to hop the gate to access the driveway. I still didn't know how I even allowed myself to be talked into that whole mess of a charade, considering that I was typically the goody two shoes out of the both of us. Not that Wes was a for real problem child, but I'd definitely been the milder mannered of us two growing up. I never wanted to step too far out of line and risk my aunt and uncle shipping me off to live in some group home somewhere, an unfounded fear that I didn't unearth until well after I'd moved out of their home and had begun seeing a therapist.

As I flipped through the *Gazette*, my eyes idly sliding across the pages, I came to a stop when an ad caught my eye. It was a full color photo of a woman who looked vaguely familiar, but I couldn't readily recall her face. What a stunningly gorgeous face it was though, smooth deep brown skin, immaculately shaped brows, slightly slanted eyes, a cute little snub shaped nose that turned up at the tip, and a sensually full set of lips.

"Who's that daddy? She looks like a queen!" Harlow said, peering over my shoulder, resting her chin on me and interrupting my cataloguing of the stranger woman's features.

"I dunno, peanut. Just a stranger in the paper," I replied, reading the words that accompanied the picture that appeared to be a personal ad of sorts.

33. SBF. Seeking SBM between the ages of 35-42. ISO the tight beat to match my perfect verse. Interested? PO Box 7158 60154.

I chuckled at the reference to *Brown Sugar* and wondered how anyone as fine as her still managed to be single and why in the hell she chose the *Gazette* of all places to run a personal ad. They had all sorts of websites and apps for whatever she was seeking to get into these days, so this choice was a curious one to say the least.

"You think she's pretty, daddy?" Harlow asked, interrupting my musing once again.

"She's *absolutely* gorgeous, peanut," I replied, finding it hard to tear my eyes from the ad.

Hours later I couldn't help but still find myself thinking about that woman in the paper and her personal ad. Something about it kept niggling at me, which was odd to say the least because I wasn't looking to get into anything with anyone any time soon. I'd just gotten in a settled routine with Harlow's presence in my life and finally settling into this career change, but that face...*those eyes* of hers had been flashing through my mind all day. I grabbed one of the copies of the newspaper to take a look at the ad again, trying to place the familiarity I felt when I looked at her, but I still couldn't put a finger on it. I also couldn't shake the feeling that I needed to reach out to her. I'd never ignored my intuition before, so instead of finishing up this order I'd planned on working through once I'd put Harlow down for the night, I found myself sitting at my drafting desk creating a response to that ad for me to drop in the mail tomorrow.

THREE

KAI

"You're not still mad at me, are you? It was an honest mistake," my cousin Tina said, standing at my front door looking completely pitiful as she clutched a handful of bags, "You don't even hold grudges. You said they give you wrinkles in *Kai's Korner* a couple months ago...so I know you're not mad."

It had been a week since I'd asked Tina to get my personal ad into the paper and she got it in there all right. Instead of it being just a plain text ad wedged between someone selling a used piano and someone else looking to give puppies up for adoption, it was a four by six-inch full color ad—with an accompanying picture. I'd never been so mortified in my life, when I grabbed a copy of the paper to ensure they'd gotten my ad right and came across my face splayed through the pages of the *Belleview Gazette*.

"Dogs go mad, people get angry," I replied, leaving the door open as I turned on a heel and left Tina standing at the front entrance of my townhome.

"You didn't slam the door in my face either, so you definitely can't be ma—*angry*," Tina continued, following me into my living room and sitting on the couch a little too close for comfort, "You can't ignore me forever, Kailene Michelle. I apologized like fifteen times. I even got Jacques to call you and apologize!"

"I just wanna know where the hell y'all even got a picture to put with the ad, Tee? All I sent you was a text. With words. Dassit!" I exclaimed, shoving her lightly away from me before I turned and pulled my legs up under me as I faced her on the couch.

"I asked Jacques where in the hell he got a photo and he claimed that he googled and that was one that came up and he thought you looked nice. He thought the lack of a photo was an oversight and you wanted the same kind of ad that you'd run in the paper before. Bright side," Tina said, holding up one finger, "he didn't charge you after realizing his mistake though!"

"You're damn right he wasn't gonna charge me for embarrassing the hell out of me in front of the whole damn town," I groused.

"Well technically our circulation is *only* about forty-three percent of the town's popul..." Tina started, but quickly amended when she saw the murderous look that I was sure was etched across my features right now, "Well...ok, you know what? Not important. Yes, embarrassed in front of whole town. Again, super mega sorry. For that. Our bad."

"Hell yeah, it's y'all bad. Would you like it if I made a mock-up of a wanted poster with your photo on it and plastered it all over town? Because y'all might as well had done that!"

"Whew, you are *truly* your mother's daughter," Tina mumbled under her breath, "I mean...how's the response so far? Any luck?"

I flung my hands toward the table in front of where we sat toward the mounds of envelopes that were stacked on it.

Tina's expression brightened, "This looks like a good twenty, thirty replies. That's an amazing response for a week's time!"

"Gon ahead pick one up and read it, sister-cousin," I said, gesturing toward the pile again, "Pick an envelope, *any* envelope..."

"Oh boy," she said, before picking up an envelope and investigating its contents, "Is this a flash drive?"

"Yes! Between half of these folks thinking I'm looking for a music producer who can catapult my aspiring rap career to success and the other half being old ass grandpas tryna shoot their geriatric game...this was a horrible idea. Why would you agree to use up one of your favors with Jacques for this? Why didn't you talk me out of this supremely stupid idea? I thought you always had my back, Tina!" I whined, dramatically falling back onto the couch and throwing my arm over my eyes.

"Nope," Tina said, pulling me back upright, "You're not putting this off one me, Kai! I tried to warn you, but your obstinate ass refused to listen to reason. You were hell bent on getting this ad in the paper. Going analog to find your woodland creature bae, or whatever the hell, who only read the paper by moonlight every third day. Now, we might have messed up the delivery of the ad, but the actual insistence and initial placement of the ad in the paper. Oh no baby girl that was *all* you. You brought this response on yourself. Period."

"Wow, who ordered logic?" I said, waving a hand frantically in the air, "Waiter...I didn't order the logic tonight."

Tina shook her head laughing at me, "Of all these replies, there is nothing good? Not one kinda sorta solid lead? I can't believe you went complete goose egg, cuzzo. I refuse."

"Well, there was one kinda sorta interesting reply," I said, rifling through the mess until I found the envelope that had just arrived today. The postmark wasn't local, so I was confused when I opened up the envelope to see a drawing that was a rendering of me, I'm assuming based on the photograph that accompanied my ad and a man sitting on a bench in the park. The back of the little card simply read "When did you fall in love with hip-hop?" So obviously the guy got my little reference in my ad, but beyond that he gave me nothing else to work with. Not even a name.

"Oh this is *cute,* Kai!" Tina squealed, "You gonna reply?"

"Reply to what? It's a *drawing*. With no name," I grumbled.

"Dude, you're buggin'! His name is right here in the corner," she said, pointing at some writing in the lower left hand of the drawing.

"Rux 2k19? I find it hard to believe that there's a man out here whose name is a campaign slogan on his birth certificate, Celestine," I replied sarcastically.

"Well duh, Kailene," she shot back, giving me just as much sass as I'd given her, "The date part isn't his name, but part of his artist tag. His name is obviously Rux. …or some variation of that. Which…is *interesting*, but also what's in a name! You have a name, an address, and a jumping off point since he got your corny little innuendo from your ad, clearly. Gon head and make this Rux fella ya lil prison pen pal or whatever. Wait…he isn't actually *in prison*, is he? What's that return address again? Can't be too sure."

I rattled off the address quickly, not even having thought that maybe he could be some dude in prison that had somehow gotten ahold of my ad. Those prison dudes did love a nice illustration to send to their lady friends if any of the shit I'd seen on Twitter was any indication.

"Oh no, he's definitely not in prison, girl. Look at this house," Tina gushed.

"How in the hell are you seeing his house?" I asked.

"Google Maps Street View, sis!" she laughed and turned her phone so we could both view what she was looking at.

She was right, "Rux's" house did look nice...very nice, in fact, for a single man to be living in.

"Why does he live in this big ass house though? He's probably someone's husband looking to creep. Ugh," I rolled my eyes, instantly irritated.

"I swear you always assume the worst. How about you at least open up the lines of communication and see what's what before you make assumptions, Kai?! Damn, I know the reason why you started *More to Life* was about being rooted in self-love before seeking love in someone else, but damn I'm pretty sure your roots are firmly implanted there, and you could afford to share the wealth of your love with someone else."

"Oh...you wanna go there?" I asked, immediately feeling like she was picking on me.

"Relax, killa. I didn't say that to rile you up. I'm just saying, stop making fire where there's no smoke. The least you can do is drop this Rux cat a note, maybe get to know him a little. Who knows where it could lead?" Tina reasoned.

"I mean you *might* have a point," I acquiesced.

Tina just shook her head at me, knowing I'd never fully concede to being wrong at any juncture. She was right though, what did I have to lose but a few strokes of a pen across paper? That was my whole thing, right? To try to get to know someone without the trappings of digital sleuthing ruining the picture for me before I'd taken a chance to actually get to know him. Getting back to the old-fashioned way of learning things about a man organically instead of finding everything I could about him on the internet and feigning surprise when he shared details that I definitely should not have known already. Dating without pre-judgement, I'd reasoned with myself, would hopefully allow me to let my guard down and actually let someone in. Not to mention, I had years and years of collected personalized stationery that had gone unused because who even used real paper anymore? Now, I guess I did.

"So…?" Tina prompted.

"You know I'm about to use you as my own personal thesaurus, right?" I asked her.

"Wouldn't have it any other way," she giggled as I got up to go to my office and grab the supplies that I needed to write this letter.

Okay, I said to myself, *I guess we're really doing this.*

I went through a smooth four drafts of varying lengths before deciding upon a few short paragraphs introducing myself a bit more and asking him a few questions in return. Tina left after round two of my drafts, swearing that I was doing the absolute most and needed to take a chill pill, but…I just…I wanted to get this *right*, you know? What exactly right entailed was far beyond my purview right now, but I knew I didn't want to come off as a weirdo or cornball, that's about all I knew for sure. Before she'd left, Tina's smart ass ensured me that it was too late for either of those options based on the fact that I'd even put the ad in the paper in the first place. But also made the very salient point that Rux had to be just as weird or cornballish to have replied to my ad in the first place. I just hoped the words I'd finally settled upon weren't too wack.

Rux—

I guess I have you at a disadvantage, knowing your name, but you not knowing mine. Wait...is that your name? Rux? I assumed from the tag on the drawing you sent that would be the safest name to refer to you by until you tell me differently. Anywho, my name is Kai...Kailene, actually, but no one calls me that beyond family when they're trying to rattle me. I'm guessing the same thing that led me to create that ad is what led you to respond, so...to answer your question...never? I'm not really too much of a hip-hop girl despite my undying love for Brown Sugar. Congrats to you for getting that reference, by the way. You're literally the only respondent to my ad so far who has gotten it. Also, not too many men would readily reveal their knowledge about mid-tier, mid-2000s Black romantic comedies, so I guess you're either a movie buff or had a former girl who forced you to watch it against your will, eh? Wow, it's too soon for me to be getting all up in your business considering that we've exchanged less than fifty words total between my ad and your reply. Which, by the way, cute drawing. Very cute. I'm guessing your talents with the pen lie less in constructing words with it and more in creating beautiful art, eh? We'll have to work on getting more words if you give if this little proposal thing is to keep going. That don't bother you, right? The letter thing...I'd just...prefer it for now. I'm way too plugged in for professional reasons, so this analog connection is my jam.

Looking forward to hearing from you soon,
Kai

I dropped the letter into a mailbox I passed on my way to pick up my goddaughter for our weekend of shenanigans. It'd been just about two weeks since Pen had put herself onto my calendar and we both were looking forward to catching up, binge watching whatever silly supernatural shows she'd found for us on *Netflix*, eating all of the worst foods, and just being in each other's company. Despite being thick as thieves, Corin and I were pretty opposite when it came to our approach at bonding with Pen. Granted, there should exist some disparity as Co was her mom and that bond wasn't one that I was fit to match. However, Corin and Penelope's bonding time was structured mainly around fitness and physical activity, while mine and Pen's time together was definitely rooted in who could meld to the couch the quickest. My one-on-one time with Pen was the only time when I let go all of my restrictions that were put into place to help me live my best life. It was just me, my best girl, and as much junk as either of our bellies could stand before one or both of us cried "uncle!" She caught me up on whatever drama was going on in her current grade and I was a listening ear, offering little to no input unless it was asked of me.

I swear it seemed like the dramatics that came along with being a tween had multiplied by one hundred in the years that had passed since I was that age compared to now. Luckily, Corin and Wes were hyperaware of the goings on in Pen's little world, so they weren't too far from the loop if any serious issues did pop off. For now, however, the older she grew, the less and less Pen confided in Corin and more she confided in me, so I had to walk the fine line of being "Cool Goddy" and also keeping her mama abreast of any foolery that was afoot.

When I arrived at *The Estate*, Corin corralled me into the east wing sitting room.

"Where's Penny?" I asked.

"She'll be down in a minute, until she is though…how's the ad thing working out? Any good leads?"

"The vast majority of them are duds, there was one with potential that Tee convinced me to give a shot. He sent the cutest little drawing, I'll have to show it to you," I said.

"A drawing huh?" Corin asked, the corners of her mouth twitching as if she was holding back some sort of amusement.

41

"I know, it sounds corny. But…it was endearing."

"No no, I didn't think it was corny at all. It sounds sweet. What's the artist's name? Maybe it's someone we know?"

"I don't think so. He isn't local. Lives out in Lakeland, which was interesting that he'd seen, let alone responded to my ad. Tina said it didn't go into the online version of the paper and their sub reach doesn't go that far."

"So, you've exchanged info with him?"

I shook my head, "Still slow rolling it. We're gonna do the pen pal thing."

"You were serious about that, huh?"

"Um, yes. You see how the last time I allowed myself to be taken in by a literal smooth-talking man panned out."

"Actually, I don't know how that panned out because you never did give me that tea, sis. You came here, drank my last split of *PJ* and then passed out, remember?"

"Oh my God. So, remember how he'd left that voicemail?"

Corin nodded and motioned with her hands for me to go on.

"Apparently, my look that night was the spitting image of his not long dead fiancé. Remember I was wearing braids then, but I guess we hadn't favored in any of the photos he'd seen of me prior to that. Anyway, that voicemail he left that evening was six and a half minutes of him going back and forth between begging me to give him another chance and crying about still not quite being over his loss. Mind you, there was no mention of said dead fiancé in any of our conversations before that, so…"

Corin's face crumpled, "So, I…he…"

"Exactly, friend. I am not equipped to unpack or process any of that. So, I politely declined returning that phone call and do wish him the best in life."

"These kinds of things only happen to you, Cobra. No one else in my life, I swear."

"So, it's me attracting the mess, great analysis Doctor CoCo. Now that we've diagnosed my defect...what's the plan for my cure?"

"You're sick, Goddy? Maybe we should cancel our plans. I can't be getting sick," Penelope suddenly piped up.

"What did I tell you about minding the business that minds you, my dear daughter?" Corin chastised.

"It's not contagious, babe. We're fine," I said to Pen, before muttering to myself, "at least I don't think it is."

Corin bit her lip to stifle a giggle.

"You ready to ride out?" I asked Pen.

She nodded and indicated the duffle bag on her shoulder. We said our goodbyes to Corin and proceeded toward the front door. I let Pen walk in front of me and before I could fully cross the threshold to get outside, Corin grabbed my arm to stop me. I lifted my key fob and pressed the button to unlock the doors so Pen could get in the car. I turned to see her grinning at me.

"Give your pen pal a chance before you write him off, okay?" she said.

"Do...you know something I don't or...?"

"I'm just saying, I know the thing with that other guy kinda had you shook and discounting yourself, but Cobra... this insistence of your gut? It isn't coincidental. It's just you finally listening to your subconscious and I hope you give it a fair shot. That's all I'm saying."

"Okay, fair enough. We'll see what happens," I replied, giving Co a quick squeeze before hopping into the car with Pen.

On the way to my house, my phone rang. My daddy's full government name flashing across the screen brought a smile to my face, unbidden. Kenneth Alexander was the only man on Earth who'd consistently been able to keep a smile on my face over the years. Not to risk sounding too much like that creepy ass song Beyoncé wrote about her father, but any man who possessed a lot of the same qualities of my father definitely would go far in the race for my heart. Kenneth Alexander was the prototype, honestly. Whenever she was nagging me about her lack of grandchildren, my mother often cited the fact that my father was too good of a man and the fact that she'd snagged him had ruined me for any real-life man of my own generation. Of course, no human was without flaw and my dad's major one was shining through once I'd answered this call.

"Hi, favorite daughter," he crooned, smoothly, "How are you today?"

"I'm your only daughter, daddy," I giggled, "What's going on?"

"So, you know your mother and aunt land from their trip today, right?"

"Mmmhmm," I replied.

"Well, okay...I'm supposed to pick them up, but see, me and Tony went out to the lake this morning to see if anything was biting and lost track of the time and..."

"Daddy," I interrupted, "What time are you supposed to pick them up?"

"Ten minutes from now," he rushed out.

"Kenneth Gregory Alexander!" I admonished, laughing.

"I know, baby girl, *I know*...I'm already gonna have to hear an earful from your mama since I won't be there, but do you think you can do your old pops a solid and snag them from the airport?" he pleaded desperately.

"I dunno," I hedged, pretending like it was an inconvenience while I had already pulled over and turned around to head in the opposite direction towards the airport, "What's in it for me?"

"My undying love and support?" my father offered.

"Already have that old man, what else?" I joked, "Nah, I'm

kidding. I got you, daddy-o. No problem. What airline are they flying again?'

He quickly relayed that he'd just sent me a text with all of the information I needed. We spoke for just a little longer to get him to agree to cover my landscaping costs for the next two months for derailing my day at the last minute. I didn't need him to do that at all, but any way to save a little extra cash? I'd take it with no complaint. When I picked up my mom and Aunt Didi, Mommy had a little bit of an attitude at it being me who came to get them as opposed to my dad, but that was quickly converted once she saw Penelope.

The drive to drop off Mom and Auntie Didi was filled with chatter as they gave us the highlights of their trip and Pen filled them in on her soccer team's past few games. I had to bite back a giggle at Mom and Auntie Didi acting like they knew anything that Pen was talking about when she used technical jargon describing her triumphs in soccer. I was thankful that we'd pulled up to their neighborhood by the time they tried switching the conversation over to me and the personal ad debacle. I certainly did not want to discuss it in front of an audience that consisted of an eleven-year-old. Penelope and I helped them out of the car with their luggage and I left with a promise to come over later in the week to dish about the latest updates in that arena. That promise was enough to hold them over for now, so I made my exit and got Pen and me to my place quickly and safely.

Once we were inside and laid out on my sectional, I ordered pizza and wings, while Penelope scrolled Netflix trying to find a new show for us to binge. Nothing caught her attention instantly, so we ended up re-watching *Charmed*, a show we'd watched all the way through at least twice already. Corin would kill me if she knew some of the more mature content that I'd exposed Pen to in our little binge parties, but nothing that was too explicit or sexual in nature.

There was only so many of those silly Disney shows I could take after so long. I was also certain that she'd watched worse with Wes, knowing his obsession with blood and gore movies.

"Goddy, do you think magic is real? I mean like…people don't really have powers like the teleportation that Leo does or how Piper can freeze things just by throwing her hands up or whatever, but sometimes…things just happen that can't be explained you know? Like there was nothing else but magic that made them possible?" Penelope asked.

"That's deep conversation, kiddo," I laughed, trying to deflect because I honestly didn't have an answer for her.

Magic was an interesting paradox to me. I didn't believe in it, but I also didn't *not* believe in it, as well. Because like Pen said, there had been too many inexplicable things in my life that have happened that were definitely tinged with magical elements that made me wonder how much of it was just life lifing or something outside of the realm of my imagining pushing things along.

"Well, I think magic is real. I mean, it's just like sprinkles of God through acts, right?" Penelope asked again.

"I…am not sure that ardent Christians would appreciate that comparison babe, but…I like it. I like it a lot. I might steal it, kid," I cracked.

"I'd like full credit if it goes in an editorial, thanks!" Penelope quipped.

"What do you know about credit?"

"Enough that if I don't provide it for sources in my research paper, I get accused of cheating and fail," Penelope sighed.

"Research paper? Don't tell me y'all are already doing those?"

She nodded, "We have a huge one due at the end of the

semester. We're supposed to pick a public figure and speak to how their influence has changed a facet of society."

"That's heavy lifting for sixth grade, sheesh," I blew out.

"*Eighth* grade, Goddy," Penelope reminded me.

I'd completely forgotten that Corin and Wes had allowed her to skip a grade and that she'd also somehow managed to start school a year earlier than she was supposed to. I'm gonna guess it was that Bellgraves name being on a few buildings at the fancy, schmancy private school that she attended that had a lil something to do with that. The same super fancy private school that her mother attended for all twelve years of her elementary and secondary education, which caused the two of us to not know one another until we'd met in undergrad despite having grown up on different sides of the same town all of our lives.

"Excuse me. Still, in eighth grade I think I was barely capable of putting more than three sentences together that made sense," I laughed.

Shaking her head, Penelope replied, giggling, "Now I know you're lying, Goddy. G-Ma showed me your magazines that you created when you were in like fifth grade or something the last time I was at her house. You been writin' *writin'* for a loooooong time."

"Dang, chill out on that elongation of the word long. I'm not that old!"

"Well compared to…nevermind, nevermind. Hey…what's this?" Penelope said, trying to quickly change the subject before she dug herself into a deeper hole.

I looked over to see what she was talking about and saw her holding up the card from Rux.

"Ooh, Uncle Teddy drew this, didn't he?" she asked, peering at the drawing, "I'd know his style anywhere!"

"*Uncle Teddy*? How do you…" I trailed off, confused.

"You didn't see him on the front page of the same paper that your pers...a...um..." Penelope abruptly stopped.

I rolled my eyes, shaking my head, knowing what she was about to say before she'd stopped herself once again.

"My what, babe?" I prompted, curious to see how she was gonna maneuver her way out of this one.

"Okay, so I mighta kinda sorta heard my mom and dad talking about a personal ad you put in the paper and how it was also in the same issue that Uncle Teddy's cover story was on and I maybe mighta took a peek to see what they were talking about...but like, I didn't even understand what the big deal was with you trying something new. Although I'm not sure if music is quite your thing, but..." Penelope shrugged.

"There are so many things here to unpack, but first...why do you keep calling him Uncle...how is Rux related to you? And do you know his actual name? Is Teddy his actual name?" I badgered Pen like I hadn't asked the man himself some of these same questions in the response that I'd finally dropped in the mail earlier today.

"*You* know Uncle Teddy, Goddy. He's my goddad. It's my daddy's brother cousin—his name Theodore, but we call him Teddy! Well, Daddy calls him The, but that's silly," Penelope replied, with more than a hint of duh in her tone.

I *knew of* Wes' brother cousin as Pen put it, but I didn't really *know* him. Theodore was the godfather counterpart to my godmother of Penelope status and at Penelope's christening years ago was probably the last time I saw him. At the time I was too wrapped up in some personal drama with my ex to pay him much mind, so I couldn't even call to mind what he looked like.

"Where the hell does Rux come from then?" I mused under my breath, more to myself than Penelope who piped up immediately.

"I asked that too because I was confused. Daddy said it was his frat name and when I asked what that meant they changed the subject really quickly so I don't think that I'm supposed to know the for real origin story of the name," Penelope frowned, "I swear you all act like I'm some kinda kid who doesn't know things."

"Or...perhaps we treat you like a kid who sometimes sticks her nose a little far in adult business like your little perusal of the newspaper?" I reminded her quickly.

"Oh."

"Yeah," I laughed, "Oh."

Just the mention of the newspaper reminded me that she said Rux was the cover boy of the infamous issue of the *Gazette* with my ill-fated ad in it. Rifling through the mess of mail and assorted items that needed to be thrown out on my coffee table, I pulled out my rumpled copy of the *Belleview Gazette* and my eyes landed on the picture of Rux immediately...Rux and an adorable cute little chocolate replica of him right in front of him. I skimmed the article, a puff piece written by this chick at the *Gazette* that my cousin couldn't stand and learned a little more about Theodore "Rux" Reed. The words in the article held my attention for far less time than the picture that accompanied the article. Rux was...*fine*. Like, *fuck this pen pal nonsense why don't you come over and see me sometime* fine.

At first glance he instantly made me think of that one night on Twitter a few years ago when the hashtag #bigguytwitter popped off because he was definitely a buffalo tender, big fine kinda fella. If I had to guess he was between six foot five to six foot seven, weighing between a smooth two hundred seventy to two hundred ninety pounds and he was solid, a legit big dude. Looking at his arms, which weren't chiseled or defined in any way, with a slight flex to them as they rested on his desk—I just wanted him to wrap me up tight and not to let me go. Arms were *kind of* my thing.

And that face...*Father Christmas*! Smooth, like it'd never seen a blemish is its life, mahogany skin. Obsidian eyes with a gaze so focused it seemed to pierce my soul right through the newsprint. A nose so negro—broadly stretched across his face, strong and wide—that I was ready to begin singing about it where Beyoncé left off. And his mouth had certainly ruined a life or three, I was convinced—two impossibly full lips, a shade slightly lighter than the rest of his skin tone with just a hint of pink showing where they met, surrounded by an impeccably groomed beard. The slight smirk into which his lips were pulled in this photo didn't get past me at all— his fine ass knew what he was doing, posing with the cute ass baby, a panty-wetting smize in his eyes, and that bearded smirk that basically dared you to come ride his face.

"Goddy, you okay? Your breathing sounds a little...off?" Penelope piped up.

I shook off the million and twelve nasty thoughts that ran through my mind about her uncle before answering, "I'm good, babe."

I threw the paper back onto my table before my thirst got even more real and had a thought that sent me directly to my phone which was charging in my room. I quickly connected with Corin.

"You set me up!" I exclaimed.

"Oh me? I'm doing fine, thanks for asking," Corin giggled.

"Girl bye, I just left your ass a few hours ago. I know you're fine. But are you gonna ignore what I just said?"

"No, I'm not ignoring it, but I also do not know what the hell you are talking about, Kai? I set you up, how? Whatever Penelope has managed to rope you into is all your own doing. I have nothing to do with it!"

"This isn't about Pen," I hissed, "It's about *Rux*."

"Why are you calling me about Teddy?" Corin asked, puzzled.

"Because somehow I know you are behind this. Setting me up," I grumbled.

"Girl, what are you talking about?"

"You didn't tell him to answer my ad because I was whining like a child about the lack of response?" I asked, pitifully.

"Uh...no. Teddy isn't the type of man who can be moved to act on anything. No matter how much fondness he holds for me."

"Whatever. I don't wholly believe you, but I also cannot prove that you weren't behind any of this either, so I guess I gotta leave it there."

"Girl...go back in there and gorge on trash with my kid 'til one or both of you call me complaining of a stomachache and leave me alone," Corin replied and hung up on me.

The nerve of her!

"Goddy?" Penelope called out, "are you sure you're okay?"

I giggled soundlessly because she sounded honestly worried and my actions in the past few minutes probably didn't help with any of that worry.

"I'm good, babe. On my way back out shortly, okay?"

"Okay," Penelope replied, skeptically, then murmured something I couldn't hear. Probably talking shit about me being crazy, which at this point was valid because I was acting strange. I needed to reel it in. I mean, it was a good thing that my people knew Rux, right? That way it was less weird that I had a stranger danger—*to me*—pen pal situation popping off that I was hoping would turn into...what exactly? I wasn't sure. But having the visual to go along with the name definitely had my mind spinning with thoughts of what it could be.

FOUR

RUX

Kai,

Nice name, it rolls off the tongue well. Pause. That didn't sound like some creep stuff, right? Because that's not what I'm on...at all...so let's just, move forward and act like I never said that. ;) To answer the inquiry about my name though, it's Theodore—Teddy to those closest to me, Rux to anyone who met me after the age of eight... but as I also .... | ! ly a (t presented me with the opportunity to obtain yet another name. I'll let you decide which of those you feel most comfortable calling me going forward, I guess.

Okay since you are not a hip-hop girl, what kinda music makes you throw your hands up and say "heyyyyyy that's my jam!"? All Black women of a certain age have at least one song that sets them off.

I'm honestly surprised that more guys didn't, or should I say haven't gotten that reference. Man, I feel like we all had to take a girl to see that joint so she could swoon over Taye Diggs and that Boris dude. It was damn near a prerequisite to getting...to know a young lady in my day, you know? And yeah it probably is too early to bring up old work as we're getting to know one another, but I definitely spent time with a young lady who wore out three DVDs of that movie from how often she watched it. I could probably quote it word for word, if pressed. (Please don't press me, ha!)

It's funny...the only way I saw your ad was because I happened to be featured in the Gazette for those drawings you called "cute", so your assumption that my talent lies in my pen for drawing is actually spot on. I'm the owner and sole operator of a custom greeting card company. My illustrations are becoming more and more sought after, which has been an exciting move for me thus far. You mentioned your job keeping you plugged into the internet and from the looks of that ad, I'm going to guess that you work in online marketing or something similar? You'll have to let me know how right I am upon your reply.

And no...the letter writing thing isn't weird. Well, okay...it isn't extra weird, but it's a smidge weird. I can dig it, though. I'll likely type up the rest of my responses instead of handwriting—beautiful penmanship, btw. If I keep subjecting you to my chicken scratch, you'd be ready to end this before it began. Taking it old school rids us of the need to do the incessant Googling and LexusNexus searching. Plus, getting to know someone the old school way could prove beneficial in actually building a rapport, so to that end, I have a few getting to know you questions to lob at you. I'll provide you with my answers to these as well, get the ball rollin', you know?

What your favorite color? Mine is black, probably somewhat of a shocker for someone whose life's work is the visual arts, but in an art class I once learned that a black object absorbs all the colors of the visible spectrum and reflects none of them to the eyes. Not to get too Hotep adjacent on you, but – I kind of like to liken that to the way I move within the world. Absorbing all the different facets of life but reflecting back into the world a wholly different view of them through my perspective.

What's your favorite drink? If we're talking nonalcoholic? Apple juice, definitely. It's the most superior of all the fruit juices and dare anyone else to object. Alcoholic? I've yet to meet a scotch that I'd kick out of bed.

What would be your dream car? Once upon a time it woulda been a sporty, two-seater coupe from some foreign car entity, but nowadays? I'm into whatever's safe and will get me from point A to B swiftly. Are you normally an early bird or operate on CPT? I am notoriously on time. So much, in fact, that my cousin who is more like my brother teases me incessantly about it.

And of course, you're having a dinner party and can invite any three folks to dine with you – dead or alive – who you got? Well, off rip I'm inviting Regina Hall (because just in case things don't work out with us? I'll have a backup. She wouldn't be able to completely fill your shoes, though!), Andre3000 (because in addition to being one of my favorite MCs that brother seems like he's hella interesting and it'd be fun to pick his brain) and my final person would be my mother (I lost her at a young age, so it would be nice to be able to see her again at my big age).

Whoa, this ended on a way more morose note than I anticipating and is already bordering on entirely too long for a second correspondence, but I wanna end on a high note, so my last question is in the movie version of your life, who would play you?

Best,
Rux

FIVE

KAI

Rux,

I'm actually really interested in the genesis of this nickname that I'll continue to call you since it was what we were first introduced as, but I guess that story will come over time, yeah? Speaking of time, I'm sure you've figured it out by now, but we've actually been acquainted for quite some time though apparently your memory is as bad as mine. We have a goddaughter in common, which should have made this a bit less disconcerting for me since I have folks that can actually vouch that you aren't some weirdo hiding a family and getting your jollies off by corresponding with me. (...you aren't hiding a family, are you?)

I've actually refrained from asking Corin and Wes much about you, preferring to...how'd you put it...get to know one another and build our own rapport. Of course, that little nosey Pen couldn't help but drop a few words about you when she and I were together. Apparently, her Uncle Teddy can do no wrong. And if Pen's on your side, you basically can't lose. One little thing though, your handwriting isn't that terrible, so...if it isn't too much of an imposition—can we keep on with the handwritten letters? Makes this whole penpal thing that much more...authentic. Indulge me. I'm new to this...ha! I'm gonna answer your little Q&A session, but I'm gonna slide back a bit further in your letter a bit to address the job thing. You couldn't be further from the truth with your guess, actually. In a way I do some internet marketing, but I also have a team that I pay very handsomely to take care of most of that for me. When you get a chance, check out moretolife.net to see what it is I do exactly. I could explain it, but it's more fun for you to find out on your own...

I'll attack your questions in reverse order. It's funny that you chose Regina Hall as your replacement for me if things don't work in our favor because she would absolutely be my choice for someone to play me in my life's story. We don't share many physical similarities beyond skin tone, but she's hella fine, smart, and funny. She'd knocking Being Kailene – the name of my autobiographical film – out the park. Not that I've given this any extensive thought or anything. :) For the dinner party—I'm going to go total cliche and say my paternal grandmother who I never got to meet because she died before I was born, Toni Morrison because she's my all-time favorite author and Beyonce because duh…c'mon, man.

As someone who has built her own empire, so to speak, and had to go through a lot of strife to get there, I absolutely believe that timeliness is closely linked to respect and people who play with your time do not hold you in high regard. Therefore, I am almost always early unless extenuating circumstances mitigate that. I could definitely see Wes Come Lately teasing you about that. Neither him nor Coco have any time awareness, which honestly drove me insane when I first met Co. It makes them perfectly suited for one another, though.

I hate driving so I don't really have a dream car, unless the answer of one that is driven by someone else is a viable option here. In a perfect world, I'd make enough money to employ a driver or luck up on a mate who didn't mind chauffeuring me hither and thither at my whim. Talk about goals! And wow, apple juice is the most superior fruit juice when ruby red grapefruit is right here? You wound me, Rux! And here I thought that you were someone I could trust. Just when you think you know a man. *smh*

This favorite color inquiry is one that trips me up every time. Not because I'm indecisive, but because for me colors have...purpose. Like there are certain ones that look better draped across my skin than others (red/yellow/gold/royal blue, for reference), others that come together to create palettes within my home that evoke emotions and feelings, and still others whose usage are employed on my website to capture attention and drive eyes to visual content. So, to that end, the entire color spectrum is my favorite because they all have distinct purpose and give me life in different ways. Wow, I'm lowkey matching your Hotep adjacent energy with my answer here, huh?

Also...I noticed that you hadn't answered the question about who'd play you in the movie of your life and...what's up with that? You don't get to lobby the Spanish Inquisition upon me then euro step answering. And along with that you can answer a few this or that questions for me...

Prince or Michael Jackson?

TLC or Destiny's Child?

Coke or Pepsi?

Beach vacation or mountain getaway?

Card games or board game?

Looking forward to your responses

Kai

SIX

RUX

Kailene,

Fine, if you insist upon having to decipher this chicken scratch, then I get full name privileges with you. Such a unique name for a beautiful woman shouldn't go largely unused.

The name thing with me isn't super deep. Theodore gave way to Teddy which gave way to Teddy Ruxpin and that was cut down to Rux. That's about the....most concise way I can explain it, really. Without talking about some....deeply embarrassing stories that also pepper the path of the name thing. I hadn't figured anything out until after Rinny's little hint for me to peruse the paper when she sent me those copies of the Gazette ran through my mind shortly after reading your letter. It's wild though, right? Zero degrees of separation and it took this to put us in contact with one another. Hopefully we progress from letters to actual conversation or it might be a little strange when we eventually run into each other at The Estate, huh?

Speaking of awkward, you couldn't give me any warning with that website, huh? Imagine my surprise when the actual name of the website loaded. Just glad that I was in the privacy of my own home and not outside because was the eggplant emoji in the logo really necessary?

The word was right there...I asked Rin about it and she said that was your story to tell, so what's up with it, girl? I hope you do know that these are all jokes and you aren't offended. Looking through the content, you've got a really solid thing going. I know all about Self Care Sundays and self-love, much respect. If you ever need a male perspective, I'm here for you. I got wellness segments in me, too.

Prince or Michael Jackson? — This is a trick question because everyone knows the answer is both.

TLC or Destiny's Child? — I know what you'd want me to say and only one of these groups contains a woman who did not burn her love's entire life down, so I'm going with H-Town's finest.

Coke or Pepsi? — Neither, honestly. Don't judge me too hard, but I'd take an RC over either.

Beach vacation or mountain getaway? — Neither, I prefer to explore cities when I take off.

Card games or board games? — Card games have been known to ruin families and lives and I'm untouchable in Monopoly, so I'm going with board games.

One last question—actually two. What in the world made you decide to put out a personal ad in the Gazette of all places? And how long are we keep up this carrier pigeon method of communication? I understand that you want to do the analog thing, but can that also not include phone calls? I've been searching the recesses of my mind trying to see if I could recall the timbre of your voice, but I can't quite pull it forward. No pressure, but when you're ready (312) 818-1982.

-Rux

SEVEN

KAI

Rux. Can you indulge me for a little longer with the letter thing? I promise you won't be in a rush to hear this voice of mine after you hear it for the first time. But I did save your

I started writing this letter and stopped...at a loss for what I was going to say next. I knew I was being silly... weird even, but this felt nice. Rux came across as very cool and down to earth, qualities that Corin reminded me that were at the top of my list in a future mate. She said that I was being ridiculous about insisting that we keep communicating by letter when I had the man's number right here. *We can vouch for him*, she insisted. *You know he ain't no sucka ass dude*, Wes championed alongside her. But when I asked the two of them about why they'd never tried to set us up previously, it was a symphony of crickets. So apparently Mr. Rux wasn't always the guy that they know and love today because their resounding silence spoke volumes. After a while I finally got them to speak a bit about his...days of being a "manwhore"—Wes' words, not mine. Apparently, Rux was very popular with the ladies and had no qualms about giving all of them a sliver of his time. Those days were behind him, I was told, but it still made me a bit...nervous when it came to this whole thing. What if I were just an abstraction for him? Someone to pass the time with, but not necessarily...build with. If my whole reasoning behind all of this malarkey with the personal ad was to actually find someone to settle with... I should probably keep my eyes open to the fact that this could be a mere...source of diversion from his everyday life. Distraction and amusement.

I picked up the pen to begin writing again but stopped and sighed instead. This was dumb. He wasn't my imagined mountain man who used letter writing as a means of communication because it was his only way and...I was delaying the inevitable. He didn't travel home a whole lot, but when it was an occasion, Rux definitely showed up at *The Estate*. And since I'd planned on slowing down for the rest of the year, it was way more likely that our paths would cross. So honestly what did I have to lose? At the worst we'd find ourselves incompatible, but still cordial. At best I could actually forge a connection that I'd been so desperately drawn to try to make. I sighed, reaching to pick up my phone instead of the pen. Fuck it, I'd call. *Or maybe I should send a text to make sure that it's a good time to call. Or maybe...*I thought before putting the phone back down on the desk and picking up the pen. We'd keep on this pen pal road until I felt it prudent to switch it up. I nodded to myself, confident in my decision until I heard Corin's voice in my head telling me that I needed to just pick up the damn phone and stop being a weirdo. So, I picked my phone up again...and scrolled to Rux's name, hitting the button to initiate a voice call before I lost my nerve. It rang three times and I was just getting ready to hang up when the line connected, and I heard a low tenor telling someone to chill before speaking direction into the phone.

"This is Rux," he said.

I was stupefied by the effect that hearing his voice had on me and I said nothing.

"...hello?"

I cleared my throat, "Uh...hey, it's Kailene. Kai...is...this a bad time?"

"Hey...uh...can you hold on for a second?" he replied.

He didn't wait for me to reply before I could hear his voice become muffled as if he had placed a hand over the phone. I could hear him talking to someone in a very conciliatory tone before he finally came back to the line.

"Sorry about that...hey, whassup, hello?"

I giggled at his silliness, "Hey..."

"So, you finally decided to use ya boy's number huh? I mean dang, took you long enough. You know these hands are how I make my living and here you go making me cramp up sending four-page letters two to three times a week. Glad you decided to cut a brother some slack..."

"Wow, so you just gonna start right in with me huh?" I laughed again, "Can I live?"

"If I know nothing else, I know that anyone who's close to Rinny can take a joke because that one doesn't know when to let up. I'm glad you used that number though...it's probably been sitting in your mailbox for long enough."

"Actually...it's been sitting on my desk *for long enough,* for your information. But all this antagonistic energy makes me wish I'd kept it on the page. Sheesh," I replied slyly.

"Well, give me a chance to change that, sweetheart," Rux shot back, smooth as hell, "So, like I said...hey whassup hello? Can I...ask you a question?"

I couldn't help the grin that spread across my face as I answered, "you just did."

"Cute," Rux said, and I could damn near see the smirk spread across his handsome, deep brown face as he said it, "Well I got *another* question then, what made you finally decide to call?"

After figuring out the mystery of who exactly Rux was, I was definitely glad that I'd kept a copy of that paper with my dreadful ad in it. And, like a creep, I'd pored over that article about him and its accompanying picture entirely too many times in the weeks we'd been acquainted.

"You want the truth?" I asked.

"Always, sweetheart."

"I heard Corin in my head calling me chickenshit."

I'm certain that wasn't the answer that he was expecting to hear as the thunderclap of laughter that left Rux's mouth was so loud that I couldn't help but join in as well. It was no use of me to try and play this cute; he had access to intel too easily—as I did on him, so I had to keep it a buck.

"Well, all right," Rux said when he'd finally sobered, "appreciate you keeping it real sweetheart. I must say that I'm glad Rinny as the devil on your shoulder worked in my favor —your voice is...not what I expected. In the best of ways."

"And yours is exactly what I'd hoped for," I laughed, causing Rux to let out another of those rumbling laughs.

"Daddy, what's so funny?" a tinny voice piped up, "I wanna laugh."

"Ah...can you give me a second, Kai?"

"Sure."

I could hear him, patiently speaking to his little one about staying out of grown folks' conversations and her trying to argue a case back. It was cute, the kid had solid points— mainly about not knowing he was on the phone because he was wearing AirPods, so he could have been watching a video or anything. For a few seconds more they went back and forth, not with the little girl responding back in a disrespectful way or anything, but that naturally inclined curiosity that came along with a child between the ages of four and six or seven. After finally getting her back settled watching what Rux referred to as "her stories", he popped back on the line.

"Sorry about this, LowLow is nosier than anything I've ever seen. I already told her that I was stepping out of the room to take a phone call, but here she comes anyway," Rux said in a way that let me know that the little one hadn't gone too far, even with his admonishment to mind her own business.

"If you need to call me back, that's fine," I said, feeling bad for encroaching on his time with his daughter.

Corin hadn't spilled all of the details about Rux, but she'd definitely told me a little bit about his co-parenting situation. It hadn't even occurred to me that he could possibly be busy with the kid today.

"Nah...you're good sweetheart. I got LOW all set up with the noise cancelling joints so she can mind *True and the Rainbow Kingdom's* business and not mine."

I giggled, "How old is she? I couldn't tell from that – mega adorable, by the way – picture of you all on the article in the Gazette."

"Harlow is five going on forty-five, determined to drive her daddy insane," Rux said, deep affection clearly lacing his tone, "I...we never really talked about her in our correspondence over these past few weeks, but I figured if me being a dad and having to co-parent would be a problem you'd've said something by now?"

"Why...would you being a father be a problem for me? Is...her mother a problem for you?"

Rux chuckled, "Nah, not at all, sweetheart. Britton and I

haven't...we don't exactly see eye to eye on anything beyond loving the hell out of our baby girl. She certainly isn't a problem for me...and won't be one for you."

"Then we're good," I replied, satisfied with that answer.

From there Rux took over the conversation, leading me down a path of talking about a whole bunch of random things that shouldn't have made sense for us to be discussing but all seemed to flow naturally. It almost felt stupid, the nerves I'd had before, after we effortlessly talked our way for damn near ninety minutes and likely would have been longer if his daughter hadn't needed to be fed. We rang off with a promise to continue our debate about which male r&b group of the nineties was superior via text.

That first conversation was all it took, honestly for us to revert to being very high schooler in our...courtship, spending a lot of time on voice calls and sending each other random texts. I liked *actually talking* to Rux a lot, he was equal parts hilarious and intelligent, with that low, rumbling voice that set off little frissons of heat in my belly. I almost never knew what was going to come out of his mouth and I liked that. Too many times before I'd dated men who... couldn't keep up, intellectually. But with Rux and I? We played off of each other, almost as if we were scene partners in an improv performance, bantering back and forth.

"What you over there grinnin' at?" my mother asked, as she, my aunt, and cousin walked up to where I was sitting waiting for them to arrive.

Mama, me, Auntie Didi, and Tina did our little *ladies who brunch* cosplay at least once monthly if I was in town. Tina and I traded off on who picked up our mothers since both of them – despite being extremely capable – refused to drive themselves unless circumstances absolutely dictated that they must. I stood to greet everyone with hugs, before leading them back inside toward the host stand so I could let the young lady working it know that our entire party was here. She led us to "our" table in a small alcove in the restaurant where we typically sat every time that we came here. It was an unspoken rule once the waitstaff noticed the frequency with which we dined here. The food was just... okay, but the mimosas were bottomless and that made it an absolute must since we didn't have very many of these places in our little suburb. I was glad to not be the designated driver today because. I was already steeling myself for being in the hot seat today.

"She must be talking to her lil prison pen pal," Tina teased.

...*and off we went*! Of course, Tina barely gave us time to have our asses in the chairs before she started in.

"Prison? I thought you said he lived out in Lakeland? Well...wait, they do have that facility down there..." my mother trailed off.

"Oh my God, Ma, he is not in prison. Your niece is joking...and not very well, I might add," I said, scowling in my cackling cousin's direction.

"So, tell us all about him," Aunt Didi pressed, "what's tea, niece?"

"Who taught you that?" Tina and I asked incredulously at the same time to my aunt's amusement.

"The same person who taught you dodge questions by firing one back—myself," she replied, eyes glinting with mirth, "So...tell us more about this...what's his name again?"

"Rux," I supplied.

"What...kinda name is that? Where his people from?" my mother piped up.

"Here...actually," I said in response to her second question, "it's actually pretty funny. He's CoCo's brother-cousin in law."

68

"Wait a minute, this is new information," Tina chimed in, "Catch me up, cousin!"

And so, I told them about how Rux was the cover boy of the edition of the *Gazette* that my ill-fated ad ran in and how he'd replied on a whim, but we didn't figure out the lack of degrees of separation between us until after my first response. I then went on to tell them about us writing the letters back and forth with that escalating to text and phone calls at this point. *Very frequent texting and calling* I thought as my phone buzzed with a message from Rux again. Tina's assumption when they walked up was right, I had been talking to him as he and Harlow were at their local children's museum once again. He was sending me photos and cute little videos of Harlow tearing through the joint. I grinned at this latest message, a selfie with Harlow's little hands nestled into Rux's beard as she kissed his cheek. I shot back a few heart eye emojis before returning to the conversation at hand.

"Okay, that's all cute and dandy," my mother said, breaking into my thoughts, "but when are you all meeting up? This pen pal thing isn't...sustainable."

"Yeah, I...it's kinda complicated," I said.

"Ooh, so he *is* hiding a family?" Tina said.

"What?" my mom, Aunt Didi and I all exclaimed at the same time.

"No!" I quickly corrected, "Why would you say that?"

"Remember...we when google mapped his address it was that big ol' house?" Tina said.

"Yes girl, however, it...he...there's no family, but he does have a daughter."

"Ah...that's the complication..." my mom said, "Baby mama drama?"

I shook my head, taking a sip of the water that the waiter had finally brought to the table, "No, actually. I haven't even officially 'met' the kid, let alone had any interaction with her mama. So, there's no issue there...yet anyway. He's assured me that there wouldn't be any issues, but the man ain't clairvoyant so I'm just...waiting. But yeah, his daughter is at his place fairly often which makes him coming here and me going there a bit difficult to maneuver."

"Isn't your job super flexible for a reason, my love?" Aunt Didi said, "It sounds to me like you're...I dunno...there's something here you're not really telling us."

"No sister dear, my child is scared to fall again is all. She *likes* this man and we all know how she doesn't really like when those pesky feelings get involved, so she's half in. Waiting for him to misstep so she can casually toss the idea of actually letting herself feel something for someone in a romantic sense to quench the unmistakable thirst that drove her to place that ad in the paper any way."

"So...you're just gonna read me like I'm not sitting right here, mommy? Really?"

"Did I stutter or lie?" she shot back right as the waiter came back with the carafes of champagne and juices before taking our orders.

I deftly dodged answering that question and moved the conversation onto a new topic because I...didn't want to talk about this anymore with them because my mother was on the edge of being too...*right*. And instead of turning this brunch into a therapy session wherein all of my business was put on front street for them to dissect and diagnose, I'd rather spend this time doing damn near *anything* else.

EIGHT

RUX

I looked at my ringing phone and immediately smiled.

"Hey auntie," I greeted sounding like Erik Killmonger.

The giggles that resounded in my ear—*my intended effect of the affectation*—made the bootleg impression decidedly less corny.

"How's my nephon today?" Aunt Lane asked.

"Wonderful now that I'm talking to you, momtie" I replied back, easily.

"Flatterer," she giggled, "So what's this I hear about you having a lil girlfriend now? I gotta hear your business on the streets these days?"

I groaned, shaking my head. I swear to God Wes gossiped more than anyone I knew. I also knew that no one but him could have updated his mama on my...situation. It wasn't really a situation *situation* since Kailene was insistent on us waiting to meet one another in person, despite having discovered that there are more than a few overlaps in the Venn diagrams of our lives. But we had been communicating for a little over a month—*progressing from*

71

handwritten letters to actually exchanging numbers—and I'd liked everything I'd learned about her so far. She was quick-witted, sarcastic, and funny. A trifecta that wasn't always easy to pull off, if I was being honest. Few people possessed the critical thinking skills to be able to do it properly.

"Now, Auntie, you know I wouldn't play you out like that! Your other son must be running his mouth out of turn again," I griped.

"Actually, I was talking to Penelope when she came out to the house last week…"

"Penelope!" I exclaimed.

Aunt Lane laughed, "I'm kidding, Teddy. It was definitely Weston Junior running his big mouth that he definitely did not inherit from me. Nope…I absolutely do not gossip, but uh…are you going to tell me about the young lady or not, baby."

"I'm sure Wes told you everything you needed to know," I grumbled.

But what Weston could not tell me was your point of view, baby. So, spit it out. You're a smitten kitten? Are you about to get Harlow a new mama?"

"Chill," I laughed, knowing that Aunt Lane wasn't the biggest fan of Britt for a multitude of reasons that had nothing to do with her.

"Mmmmhmmm, you ain't slick, but I'ma let you live like you kids say. Don't think I haven't noticed how you're being really tight-lipped. You must like this one. She's a nice girl. A *good* girl."

"She's cool."

"Cool. Yeah, okay, sure, baby. Just let me know when I should look out for the Rux Original invite that should be in the mail soon," Aunt Lane laughed.

I shook my head again, "You and your son wildin', auntie,

ain't no wedding bells sounding off. I haven't even physically been in her presence."

A gripe that had been plaguing me ever since I realized why she looked so familiar in the first place when I saw her ad in the *Gazette*. But that would all be changing pretty soon as Harlow and I were driving down to see the fam for Aunt Lane's surprise birthday party that was being held at Wes and Corin's place this weekend. I made sure to not only ensure that Kailene was invited, but that she accepted said invitation by a little bit of badgering on my end that I hoped she hadn't found too intrusive.

"Oh please, you'll see her soon enough. Like tomorrow at the lil party I have to act like I'm shocked to know about, but that has been meticulously planned by me using my husband as proxy," Aunt Lane laughed again.

I should have known that they couldn't get anything past her. Hell, I wouldn't be surprised if she put Uncle Weston up to getting Wes and Corin to think that the idea for it all was theirs. Those two were a complete mess.

"What party?" I asked, feigning ignorance.

"You don't lie well, baby. I already know when you and Harlow are pulling in, down to the minute. I don't know why your brother and his wife think they're really pulling the wool over someone's eyes, but if they wanna play these games, I guess I can go along to get along."

"You know you a mess right, auntie?" I chuckled.

"One y'all can't get enough of...so, you're really not gonna talk to me about Kai at all? Really, Teddy? I thought we were better than that!"

"Aight, I'll bite...what you wanna know?"

"Does she know about Harlow? Is she okay with possibly becoming a stepmama? Is she aware that your baby mama is a complete bi...bothersome woman? Do either of you find it weird that it took a personal ad to bring you together despite

73

having less than one literal degree of separation?" Aunt Lane rushed out in one breath before trying to continue before I stopped her.

"Yooooo…you really did have a whole list, huh?"

"I mean, I may have had a few inquiries that briefly crossed my mind before I decided to call you," she giggled.

"Like I said…a mess. But look, I'm not really up for the Spanish inquisition right now, so I'll cap it all off by saying this and then I gotta go," I said, peering at the wall clock in my office, "I need to leave to grab LowLow from her mom soon before we get on the road. Kailene is…she and I…what I'm trying to say is…I'm trying not to fuck it up, auntie. Yes, she knows about baby girl and we haven't expressly talked about the future or anything, but I know she's just as excited to finally make her acquaintance as well as mine. Which, honestly, just endeared her to me even more. I'm enjoying getting to know her and am looking forward to that connection growing once we move into this next stage of whatever we're doing here."

Aunt Lane sighed, "Well, this is *refreshing*. I was certain you were going to tell me to mind my business again, but… you…okay. *Okay*."

"Wait…" I said, curious about her lack of a second round of questioning, "You ain't got nothing else to add? To ask?"

"Nah-uhn. There's nothing else I need. For now," Aunt Lane replied, cryptically.

"Okay now what does that mean?" I asked.

"Oh nothing. All right baby, I ain't gonna hold you up for too much longer, I know you gotta go get my dumplin' from that bi…bothersome woman. Give her a big ol kiss from her Lolly and tell her I can't wait to see her. Love you," Aunt Lane rushed out before disconnecting the call.

"Love you, too," I said to the dead air, while shaking my head, "What the *hell* was that?"

On my way to pick up Harlow I decided to give Wes a call so I could give him shit for gossiping about me with his mama like a little girl. My call, however, went unanswered, which was strange for Wes because I didn't know anyone who was permanently glued to their phone more than he was. I bet Auntie rushed off the phone with me so she could gossip with his ass some more. Which meant my weekend in Belleview would definitely be some shit. I just hoped that none of it would hit the fan in front of Kailene. As if she knew I was thinking about her, my phone dinged with a text from her.

Let me know when you've got LowLow. I need her help. — KBae ♥

You gon stop using my baby. What did you do before she came along?

Gave Amber, my nail tech, a huge headache every time I came in for a fill is what I did. But wow, you already tryna come between me and my little friend. SMH. Ain't there something in the Bible about a jealous spirit? — KBae ♥

I know you're on your way to get her, you might as well just FaceTime me as soon as she gets in the car. My appointment is in an hour. — KBae ♥

I barked out a laugh.

You're really serious, huh?

Yes, she's my little color genius. — KBae ♥

Daddy gets no say so? Cold world.

You remember how this all came about in the first place right? ;) — KBae ♥

Laughing out loud again, I certainly did. I hadn't planned on introducing Kailene and Harlow as soon as I did at all.

But, one weekend LowLow was with me instead of her mom and when I thought she was napping, I was laid up in bed on FaceTime with Kailene who couldn't decide on a nail color. She'd been teasingly pressuring me to help her make a decision when out of nowhere Harlow popped up and made the decision for the both of us, which led to what should have been an awkward introduction except my baby girl had inherited her daddy's ability to charm the pants off anyone she met, so it went smoother than I'd thought. I'd expected Kailene to be thrown off by how everything unfolded, but she was unbothered, easily falling into conversation with Harlow about nail polish. I'd ended up having to bring the conversation to a close between the two of them after about ten minutes because...well I was feeling left out.

Touché. We'll call you in about twenty.

:) — KBae ♥

Navigating out of my thread with Kailene, I shot Britton a quick text to let her know that I'd be pulling up to their house shortly so our handoff of Harlow would be smooth. She still hadn't replied by the time I pulled up, so I hopped out of my truck hoping that Harlow would be ready to go when I rang the bell. Britton answered the door after a long pause with a stank attitude. *Here we go,* I thought. I had no idea what had set her off since we'd actually been getting along fairly well since her impromptu switch up on me. Ok, *well* was a stretch, but there was definitely markedly less animosity between the two of us, something even Harlow noticed and commented on. This frosty reception today, however, looked to be a signal of the end of whatever unspoken truce Britton had reconciled with me in her brain.

"LowLow ready?" I asked with a grin, trying to keep my tone light, despite being irritated at the fact of her ignoring my text and currently blockading the door barring my entrance.

"Before y'all take off can we chat?" Britton asked icily.

"Yeah...you gonna let me in or...?" I replied casually, humor clearly lacing my tone.

Britton rolled her eyes before sucking her teeth and stepping backwards into the house, heading towards her living room. She left the door open, presumably, for me to follow. I scratched my head, genuinely confused about whatever the hell was going on now.

"Is something wrong, Britt? Everything good with Low?" I asked once I'd sat on the couch across from Britton.

"Who's Miss Kai?" Britton shot back.

Oh shit, here we go, I thought. This attitude all made sense now. Seems like Harlow had been running her little mouth a bit.

"She's a family friend," I replied, trying to avoid this escalating into something more than it needed to be.

"Oh? Because according to my daughter she's daddy's girlfriend. You didn't feel that you needed to tell me that you're going to be having my daughter around bit...other women?" Britt gritted out, almost as if she were trying to restrain herself from flying off the handle.

"You mean how you told me about ol' boy before taking my baby away for the weekend with buddy?" I shot back, defensive for no apparent reason.

"You knew I was dating," Britt replied, "But we're not talking about me right now. We're talking about you. And *Miss Kai*. With whom my daughter seems awfully familiar. And extremely excited to be around this weekend."

"Britt—you know we're going back to Belleview for Auntie's birthday. Stop trying to make this into something it's not."

"So, you're not going to have my daughter around some stranger woman that you have never felt a need to introduce to me or even bring up her name in casual conversation?"

"When do we ever have casual conversation, Britton? We talk about our daughter and that's it."

"And this concerns my daughter!" Britt yelled.

"Our," I said, quietly.

"What?" Britt snapped.

"Our daughter. You keep saying my my *my*. She's *my* daughter, too. And she'll be around Kailene, who is *not my girlfriend* for the record, just the same amount of time she'll be around anyone else that weekend. So, I didn't feel a need to bring special attention to them spending time together. Should I reach out to Wes and Corin to get the guest list so you can have a running tally of everyone Harlow will come into contact with at the party, too?"

"Ok, now you're just being ridiculous," Britt sighed.

"Nah...only one of us is being ridiculous here and it ain't me. Harlow," I called out, "Let's boogie!"

"I wasn't done talking to you, Theodore Reed," Britt said.

"This...conversation wasn't going anywhere, anyway, Britt."

"Look, don't be out here playing house with some bitch and getting my daughter attached when we both know she won't be around for long anyway, if your track record has anything to say about it."

"And there it is. Here you go with this bullsh—" I started, before quickly truncating the rest of my sentence as I saw Harlow peeking around the corner with her little Doc McStuffins luggage in tow.

"You guys fighting again?" Harlow sighed, as she walked into the room to stand near me.

I picked her up, propping her on my side and maintained eye contact with her, "Nope, peanut. You mommy and I just have a slight difference of opinion. No fighting. Now...are you ready to see Uncle Wes, Auntie Rinny, Penny, Lolly and Pop?"

Harlow grinned broadly and nodded vigorously as expected, "And Miss Kai too, right daddy?"

"Yes, peanut, Miss Kai will be at your Lolly's birthday party tomorrow, too," I replied.

"YAY! Don't forget we gotta go gets my nails did so mine can be cute like Miss Kai's," Harlow said, matter-of-factly.

Fuck, I hissed under my breath as I heard Britt grumbling words of discontent. The kid definitely wasn't helping this awkward situation get any better. Setting Harlow down on her feet again, I nudged her toward her mother, "Go give mommy a big hug and kiss and tell her you'll see her in a couple days."

At my directive, Harlow immediately ran toward her mama and Britt fixed her expression into something more pleasant as she received all of baby girl's loving before we took off. I hit the power locks on the truck and told Harlow to hop in while I finished up with her mama.

"Just for the record, not that I have anything to prove to you, but you have nothing to worry about with Harlow getting too attached to Kailene if she and I don't work out because she'll be around regardless. She's Corin's best friend and..."

"Oh, and isn't that convenient," Britt sniped, cutting me off.

I sighed, then scrubbed a hand over my head, "Never mind BM, you got it. We'll see you Sunday."

"Make sure my...*our* baby calls me nightly please," Britt demanded.

"Whatever man," I replied, throwing a hand over my shoulder.

I buckled Harlow in securely before getting into place and backing out of the driveway.

"Daddy?" Harlow called out.

"Yeah, peanut?"

"Is mommy mad at me?" she asked in a small voice.

"What? Noooo. Mommy's not mad at you at all, peanut. Why would you think that?" I asked.

"Earlier when I was talking to her about our trip she used the s word to me. And she always told me to never say the s word, even if I was real mad," Harlow said, "I think she's mad. But I dunno why."

"The s word?" I asked.

"Yeah, you know. Sh—shu—shut...when you want somebody to be quiet."

I had to bite back a laugh because I definitely had a different s word in mind.

"Mommy's not mad at you, baby girl. She was just a little frustrated with Daddy, is all," I replied back soothingly, "If she was mad at you, would she have given you big hugs and kisses before we left?"

Harlow shrugged, "I guess not."

"I know not!" I replied, before being interrupted by my phone ringing. Glancing at my dashboard, I grabbed the handset and held it back within Harlow's reach. "That's for you, kid!"

She grabbed the phone, "Oh it's Miss Kai!"

Swiping to connect the FaceTime request, Harlow answered swiftly and I could tell Kai was taken aback by the kid answering and not me, but she recovered quickly, presenting Harlow with the color choices she'd narrowed it down to before she went into the nail shop. They chatted back and forth for a few minutes before Harlow tried handing the phone back to me at Kailene's request. I grabbed the phone and put it in the mount on my dash before speaking.

"Orange, huh?" I said, laughing, "Bet you wasn't expecting that choice."

"Actually, it's a really cute color," Kailene replied giggling, holding up the swatch so I could see it.

Nail polish was nail polish to me, so I feigned excitement which Kailene picked up on immediately.

"You know, for someone who is an artist, I'd think you would hold a deeper appreciation for the breadth of the color spectrum, man! Sheesh!"

I shrugged, "Meh..."

"Tough crowd," Kailene clucked, which made me chuckle.

"I mean, anything you put on looks good, sweetheart, so..."

"Smooth, real smooth clean up, Mr. Ruxpin," Kailene replied, grinning.

I groaned, "I hate that I even told you the genesis of my nickname when you leverage it against me like that."

"Whatever, you know you love it when I say your name..." Kailene crooned sultrily.

"Aye, relax. There's children present, girl," I laughed, "Don't start none, won't be none."

"I'ma let you go. I gotta be at Amber's in ten minutes and I'm already running behind. See y'all when you touch down, okay?"

"Aight. Until then."

"Daddy?" Harlow piped up again.

"Yes, peanut?"

"Why did you tell mommy that Miss Kai ain't your girl-friend. You called her sweetheart. Didn't you tell me that's something that boyfriends call their girlfriends sometimes?"

This kid and her damned questions.

"What did I tell you about little ears paying too close attention to adult conversation?" I asked.

"I couldn't help it. I'm right here!" Harlow replied innocently.

"You weren't right there when I was talking to your mother though," I said.

"Oh. Yeah. Whoops, I forgot."

"Likely story, kid," I chuckled.

"But daddy, are you gonna answer my question?"

"Is it any of your business?"

"Well, not really."

"And what does daddy always tell you about business?"

"To mind my own. But daddy, I don't have no business."

I bit my lip to stifle my laughter, "You got plenty business, peanut. None of it concerns me and Miss Kai or your mommy, okay?"

"Okay, daddy. But...just so you know...I know Miss Kai is your girlfriend. And I'm glad because she's nice...and pretty."

"All right, peanut. You got your tablet, right? Don't you wanna watch something until we get to Uncle Wes' house?" I asked, desperate to switch this conversation onto something else because I didn't know where this conversation would lead.

"Okay, daddy," Harlow agreed, letting me off the hook a lot easier than I thought she would.

The few hours it took for us to travel to Belleview flew by and we were pulling into Wes and Corin's estate in next to no time. At some point Harlow's television shows began watching her because she was completely knocked out when I pulled into their circular driveway. I called Wes quickly to get him to carry her inside while I parked and grabbed our bags to bring them inside.

"Uncle Rux, you need some help?" Penelope called out, walking out of the front door as I made my way from the garage to the foyer.

"Nah, I'm good, lil bit. Did your dad send you out here?"

"Yep," she replied, rolling her eyes, "Something about earning my keep."

I laughed shaking my head; that shit sounded just like Wes. He had a little bit of a complex about his kid growing up with a platinum spoon in her mouth, so he invented ways to make her "work". Never mind that it was wholly unnecessary because despite being privileged in ways that we could not even have fathomed as kids, Penny was *mostly* down to earth.

"But," she started, "While I've got your attention. I have a few revisions for the draft of the drawing you sent me last week. You got a minute?"

"Let me get all this stuff settled in our room and then I'm all yours kid," I replied, glad that I had thrown my sketch book inside of my bag at the last moment.

Something told me that this would happen. Especially since Penny's favorite word "vibe" had been replaced with "aesthetic" when she and I initially chatted about her project for me. Apparently, she was big into the 80&90s hip-hop aesthetic and wanted that reflected in the theme for the custom artwork she'd commissioned from me in addition to the custom invites. Word on the curb was that Kailene had been roped into this circus too—given the role as Penelope's key stylist for her pre-party photoshoot and the actual party's outfit, too. I was grossly unaware that twelve was such an important birthday but was quickly informed that *every single one* of Penelope's birthdays was *gravely* important.

I just thanked my lucky stars that we could still get away with paying for ten to twelve kids at whatever local funtertainment complex was popping in our area at the time for Harlow's parties. I was not looking forward to dealing with aesthetics and mood boards when it came to my own kid any time soon. I jogged back downstairs to see that Penelope had dragged out the mood boards I'd seen numerous times over FaceTime with a few addenda.

"I know Lolly's party is why you're here this weekend, but

I figured you could walk and chew bubble gum at the same time so, here we go," Penelope said, before launching into her spiel about a whole damned graffiti wall that she wanted me to create from scratch for photo ops at her party.

As she was wrapping up, Wes walked into the room and I cracked, "I hope you have enough money to pay for whatever your daughter calls herself talking me into right now."

"Oh please, everybody knows Uncle Teddy is a pushover for his goddaughter. I ain't worried. You'll cut me a deal," Wes laughed.

"I'm gonna send you pics of these updated boards, okay, Uncle Teddy?" Penelope said, walking out of the room.

"Aight, Penny," I replied to her retreating back and turning to stare at her father who was looking at me like the cat who ate the canary, "Wes, why are you looking at me like that?"

"Oh, you know why I'm looking at you like this," Wes replied smugly.

"I actually don't and it's a little unnerving, g," I chuckled.

"So, you and Kai, huh?"

"You wanna grab a brush so we can braid each other's hair while we have this conversation or nah?"

"Man, shut up! I gotta say I'm surprised though, bro. I thought you were focusing on building the brand and not in the space for a relationship. Or was that just the party line you sold Britt to let her down easy," Wes asked.

"G, don't even say her name right now. She ain't my favorite person right now. You know she was acting a damn fool when I went to go pick up LowLow. Straight up tight about us coming down here and Low being around Kailene."

"Bruh, you can see both sides of this though right?"

"What are you even talking about, man? Ain't no sides of anything."

"Just six short months ago you told your baby mama

wasn't shit shaking for a relationship anytime in your near future only to end up on ya Ella Mai shit with a shorty now. And you don't see why she tight?"

"Maaaaan, Britt already knew what it was, though," I reasoned.

Wes shook his head, "Nah, bro. Let's not act like you're the innocent party here. You gotta own your shit, too."

"What are you even talking about, Wes?" I asked, exasperated.

"Were you or were you not fucking on Britton shortly after finding out about Harlow?"

"I..." I hedged, rubbing the back of my head, "dawg...what does that have to do with anything now? We had an understanding then...and now. Like I said, Britt knew what it was. What it's always been between us. I love my peanut and wouldn't change the world not to have her here, but me and Britt were never on no real shit, G. Everybody knew that."

"I don't know if *she* knew that. Logically she did, but you blurred the lines a hell of a lot back in the day. She mighta thought shit was different than it actually was. Hell, you *know* she thought she was different with the whole not telling you about a baby for three and a half years of her life because you made it abundantly clear that you wanted nothing to do with relationships, kids, families, and all of that shit well after she was far enough along to have an abortion."

"Wes, please. You say that like I willingly misled Britt into thinking some shit was something it wasn't, though. I didn't even know she was pregnant and then she went ghost on me, so...again, I fail to see your point here. Also, she got a whole man over there. Why is she worried about what's going on with me and mine?"

"Oh...so there is a mine when it comes to Kai, huh?"

"Relax, don't go running to your diary to gush over me

finding my one twue wuv quite yet, bro. I'm just saying, Britt gotta mind her business."

"Anything that involves *her child* is *her business* though, bro."

"My relationship or lack thereof doesn't involve *our child* though," I shot back, "The only thing she needs to be concerned with is whether or not I am there for Harlow when she needs me."

"I get that, bruh. I honestly do. But, you gotta realize that your relationship...that you refuse to acknowledge but we'll come back to that...isn't in a silo, man. There's overlap. Hell, you already said that Kai and LowLow are bonding and shit. You don't think her mama has a right to know about new people you're bringing in your child's life? Where they do that at?"

"She ain't tell me about that dude tho!" I yelled.

"He preceded your reappearance in their lives, The," Wes tried reasoning.

"And then he got ghost when I started coming around. She ain't mention shit about him being a permanent fixture in their lives again. I had to hear that shit from my baby girl."

"And that was Britt's bad. So is you not telling her about Kai your way of exacting petty revenge?"

"Nobody was not telling that girl nothing, Weston Junior. It just ain't much to tell yet, G. That's it. Kailene and I are still in the very early stages of navigating through whatever we're doing here. If it becomes something serious, then that's the time for Britt to get informed about anything. But until then..." I shrugged.

"Aight man, you got it. I ain't gonna argue any further back and forth with you about this. Hell, that ain't even why I brought Kai up!"

"Yeah, you prolly brought her up so you can run back to your mama with some more gossip, huh?" I jeered, laughing.

"Look, how my mother and I bond is none of your business," Wes chuckled, "Weren't you just talking about people minding their business?"

"I know you didn't," I replied laughing as Corin walked into the house, "Rin, get your husband, sis!"

"He was your brother first! Whatever trouble he's causing that's all you, bro," Corin replied quickly, coming over to give me a quick hug, then demanding that both Wes and I come outside to unload her car.

She was coming back from a last-minute run for party supplies and had overdone it. For some reason, she had not hired a planner for Aunt Lane's party, insisting that instead of paying someone money to handle things she could do it all. Since the affair was relatively small, no more than thirty guests, I had no doubt that Corin could handle everything, but...I wondered why. I quickly found out as Wes and I unloaded the car and he got to fussing about Corin doing too much trying to impress his mama. I didn't know what that was all about since Aunt Lane loved Corin more than me and Wes combined, it seemed, but that was something me and him could rap about later. For now, we were Corin's minions for the rest of the night; helping her with setup that Penelope and Kailene would be helping complete tomorrow. Just the thought of her name brought a grin to my face unbidden.

Tomorrow we'd finally be meeting face to face for the first time since we saw each other at Penelope's christening way back in the day. I couldn't front, I was a little bit nervous since I didn't know how it would be in person. I mean, we'd definitely fallen into a distinct groove and *vibe*, to use Penny's term, over the past few weeks, but it was easy to do that when you were in a controlled environment of using written communication as your main way of interacting. I just hoped all of those hours of letter writing and texts would convert into an easy camaraderie once we were finally face to face.

NINE

KAI

"Where the hell are you?" Corin yelled into my phone moments after I swiped it to answer.

"At home?" I replied.

"I thought you were coming over for breakfast. Had your boy over here pressed staring a hole in my front door waiting for your arrival," she laughed, "And that's after he called himself being Chef BoyarTeddy over here making waffles from scratch and everything. Girl tell me how you got this man whipped and he ain't even got a whiff yet!"

I tried joining her in laughter, but it came out sounding like an awkward robotic bark.

"Cobra...what the hell was that? Are...you okay over there?" Corin asked.

"I...I think I don't feel well," I whispered into the phone, "I'm not gonna be able to make it to the party."

"Oh no, what's wrong?" Corin asked.

"Fever, throat thing," I whispered again, kind of shocked that she was buying this paper-thin ass story I was making up on the fly.

"Lemme send your man over with some medicine to give

you some up close and personal TLC then, chica," Corin replied, "Teddy!"

"No, no," I fake coughed, "I don't want to give him my germs."

"You are so full of shit, Kai. You think I really can't tell your ass ain't sick? What's really going on?"

I sighed, speaking in my normal tone, "Truth bomb? I'm scared to come face to face with Rux. Yes, me, the queen of empowerment and whatever other bullshit I've fleeced people into believe I actually practiced in my real life all these years is a sham. Go after what you want. No one can stop you but you! It's all a lie. I mean how do you even know what you want is what you need? Or good for you. Or—"

"Whoa, Cobra. Calm down. Breathe!" Corin replied soothingly, a hint of a giggle in her voice.

"You think this is funny? This is a game to you?"

"Wow, you're really spiraling over there. Awwwww, you really like Teddy, huh, Cobra?"

I groaned into the phone, "This is stupid, Co. Supremely foolish. He's just a guy, right? No big deal. It's fine. And we both know *I'm fine*."

"You know what's not fine? You not already being here to finish helping me set up for this stupid dinner for twenty people that I let my father in law and husband talk me into to celebrate my lovely, but let's face it hella picky mother in law," Corin whined.

"Nope, we both can't be having breakdown crises at the same. It's against the rules," I whined right back.

"There's only one way to solve this," Corin said, then hung up the voice call.

I laughed—a real one this time—when I realized that she hung up on me to initiate a video call.

"Rock, Paper, Scissors," she said once we could see one another, "It's the only way."

"Ugh, fine," I agreed, propping my phone up on my vanity mirror, "Best of three. And don't cheat saying it was a technical difficulty either, heffa!"

Corin cackled loudly, "Hey! I don't cheat!"

"A lie! C'mon so we can see whose breakdown is the most important. One, two, three...shoot!"

Three quick rounds later, two of which were lost by me, and I was listening to Corin vent about how stressed this party tonight had her. I wisely refrained from telling her that I believed that it was all self-driven stress. Mainly because I'd been around her mother in law several times and she always seemed pretty laid back and low key. The way Co was stressing about everything being perfect for this dinner tonight, you would think that she was preparing for a visit from The Queen Mother herself.

"Look...are you coming early or am I about to alienate this man who lives in this house with me as I turn into a hostesszilla and ruin the rest of his morning and afternoon?" Corin sighed, "I just need to prepare myself...and him for whatever the outcome of your decision ends up being. Your man isn't even here if that helps."

"Wait...what do you mean, he's not there? He told me that they were when we were texting earlier."

"Yeah, well Harlow was badgering him about going to *get her nails did for Miss Kai* and he said something about getting his lining touched up, so him and the girls are off doing that," Corin replied, "Does this mean you're coming?"

"I..."

"Listen you won't have time to be nervous with all of the shit I'm about to have you doing, so bring your ass, girl. And pack a bag, you know how you get."

"I...want to be offended but, you're right. Ugh, fine. Fine!" I whined.

"I don't really understand what has you so scared anyway.

Like you ain't been talking to this negro day in and out for what? Something like six weeks now?" Corin laughed.

"I...we...that's not the same. You know I'm so much better in writing!" I exclaimed.

Corin shook her head laughing at me, "So I'll see you in twenty? You look mad cute, by the way..."

Despite having cold feet, I had gotten up this morning and played around with the flexirods in my hair. The result actually was super cute, which alleviated some of my stress, but not quite enough to spur me on to make my way to Corin's house.

"Fine," I sighed reluctantly, "see you in twenty."

I was already fully dressed, with the bag Corin had mentioned me packing already put together, so it took me no time to get out of the door. By the time I'd shown up, Corin had managed to work herself up into a tizzy once again, so as soon as I crossed the threshold of their door, Wes peaced out —stealing away to his little man cave across the house from where we were currently stationed in the dining room. The food was gratefully being catered, so all we really had to do was decorate and set the ginormous table in the formal dining room. After a little bit of talking and a couple of glasses of bubbly, Corin had calmed down and we got to work. Corin's mother in law Elaine was turning sixty-five and had a fondness for...flair and rose gold. Both of those things were evident in the custom-made decorations, name plates at each place setting and even the china and glasses that Corin chose to use for this evening.

"Mamaaaaaa," Penelope called out.

"I'm in the dining room, Bug!" Corin called back.

My chest immediately seized because if Pen was back that meant so were Rux and Harlow. It was much easier to put everything out of my mind without their presence in the house, but now...I took another deep breath and looked around for the bottle of water I'd been sipping from as we worked. Soon I heard the pitter patter of feet too little to belong to Pen.

"Auntie Rinny look at my naaaaails," Harlow said, running into the room and launching herself onto Corin's lap.

Penelope entered the room shortly after her, coming over to give me a hug before going over to her mom to show off her manicure as well.

"Ooh, they look like little flowers, LowLow. How darling! Look, Kai, you guys are matching!" Corin said.

At the sound of my name, Harlow's little head whipped around to the other side of the room where I'd been standing silently taking it all in.

"Miss Kai, you're here!" Harlow squealed, sliding out of Corin's lap and running straight into my legs, hugging me tightly.

I bent over to embrace her back instinctively, a little taken aback by her enthusiasm, but quickly absorbing it. I peeled her little body away from my legs so that I could kneel down and get eye level with her.

"Let me see these nails, little mama!" I said, enthusiastically.

Harlow responded just like I thought she would, fanning her fingers out in front of her body, wrists bent and giving a perfect pose for a post-manicure shot.

"Oooooh, how pretty. I love your nails, Harlow!" I gushed.

"I wanted to get orange nails like you Miss Kai. So, we could match! My daddy said orange don't match my dress for Lolly's party, but I don't care."

I chuckled, "I'm sure you'll work it out, and look fabulous, Harlow."

She grinned, her tongue sticking through her teeth, clearly basking in the compliments. That basking lasted about thirty seconds before she took off running down the hall back toward where her dad and Uncle Wes were, I was certain.

"Okay stepmom!" Corin whispered, coming to stand alongside me and poking me in the shoulder.

I rolled my eyes, "Relax, Co."

"I'm just saying, somebody abandoned her favorite auntie for Miss Kai awfully quickly," Corin teased.

I felt my face getting hot as I brushed her teasing off. Some of my nervousness definitely had to do with how Harlow would take to me in person, so to have her embrace me so quickly and lovingly definitely took a modicum of stress off, but I was still pretty tightly clenched. Corin nudged me to follow her and Pen out of the dining room and into the common area where I could hear Wes and Rux going back and forth.

"Man, if you don't get your big ass out the mirror. You still the fairest one of them all," I heard Wes teasing as we walked into the room.

"Man, I'm tellin' you, buddy messed up my lining," Rux groused as he hunkered in front of a small decorative mirror that hung in the hallway between the dining room and living room.

Summoning courage from the depths of my soul I sauntered up behind him and whispered into his ear, "Yeah, it does look a little higher on the left."

Rux froze briefly before turning around, his gaze wide and his grin wider. He quickly embraced me—*tightly*—damn near picking me up completely off the ground. All of that previous anxiety I held dissipated once I was in the safety of his arms. The only thing I felt being this close to him was tingly and fluttery.

He emitted a low growl directly into my ear, "Whassup, Kailene."

"Hey," I said softly, relishing the feel of being wrapped up in Rux's arms.

He squeezed me tightly once again before letting me go slightly, putting a little bit of space between us.

"It's so good to...*see* you. So good," he said before wrapping me up in a hug once again.

"Damn bro, you gon let the girl breathe or nah?" Wes called out, causing everyone in the room to laugh.

Rux finally let me out of his embrace, but didn't let me get too far, keeping my hand encased in his as we stood there grinning at each other stupidly.

"Daddy, Miss Kai said my nails were pretty!" Harlow piped up.

"Because they are, peanut!" Rux replied, amused.

"But you said they don't match my dress!" she pouted.

"That doesn't mean I don't think they're pretty, baby girl," Rux said.

"You guys should take a walk!" Corin said, suddenly.

I turned to look at her, wondering what the heck she was talking about.

"Babe, I thought you wanted Kai to hel—" Wes started before she elbowed him in the side.

"LowLow, come and help me finish setting the table for Lolly's dinner tonight," Corin said, grabbing Harlow by one hand and walking back towards the dining room while shooing Rux and I away with the other, "Go look at the garden. It's beautiful right now!"

I allowed myself to be pulled out of the room by Rux who, apparently, had some sort of understanding of whatever Corin was getting at while poor Wes looked just as confused as I was. My confusion quickly gave way to clarity when, as soon as we crossed the threshold of the foyer near the front door, Rux pulled me into him again, joining our mouths in one hell of a kiss. I was caught off guard by the swift motion, but quickly adjusted, bringing my hands up to cup his face as our tongues battled one another before we separated to catch our breaths.

"I've wanted to do that for at least six weeks," Rux murmured, his lips still close enough to mine that I felt as well as heard his words.

"Apparently I should have been wanting you to do that for the past six weeks," I replied, reaching up to pull him back down to my level and connect our lips once again.

We stood there making out like teenagers for a few minutes more before Rux pulled back, staring down on me with his lower lip pulled between his teeth. I felt my face grow warm under his perusal, glad for the medium brown hue of my skin masking the redness that certainly accompanied my embarrassment from him just staring and not speaking.

"What?" I asked after it'd been over two minutes of him staring and saying nothing.

"I'm just...taking it all in, committing to memory..."

"Oh my god, you act like you're never going to see me again."

"Nah," Rux said, shaking his head, "I'm definitely seeing your pretty ass as often as I can, sweetheart. Trust that."

I grinned and shook my head at myself for ever being nervous about this meeting in the first place. I'd only been around Rux for a few minutes so far, but I felt *good*. Better than I'd felt in the company of a man in quite some time. And it was more than the fact that I was so attracted to him that my pussy had been performing a Sheila E drum solo ever since he first pulled me into an embrace. I couldn't quite explain the sense of...calm that he evoked in me, just being in his physical presence. We stayed outside for a few minutes more, just soaking up being here—together—in this moment before I headed back in to help with the last-minute preparation like I was supposed to be doing anyway. As soon as I stepped back into the dining room, Corin made a beeline in my direction.

"So?"

I clapped my hands together, "What else is left to do?"

"Really?" Corin said, resting her hands on her waist.

I nodded over to Penelope and Harlow who both, despite looking like they weren't paying attention to us, were keenly tuned into our conversation. And I wasn't debriefing in the presence of kids. Corin and I could chat later. She caught my vibe quickly and we both set about picking up discarded decoration encasements and straightening up the room before heading to get changed for the actual soiree.

Despite all of her earlier nervousness, when it came to hosting Corin was the face of perfect peace, greeting everyone who arrived with an air of regality, refusing to hire staff beyond the valet who was charged with hiding cars and disappearing once Corin's in-laws were known to be in the vicinity. As far as her mother in law knew, she was just coming by their home for a lowkey family dinner with her boys, Corin, and their kids. Instead, what she'd be walking into was a lavishly extravagant party with over twenty of her closest friends and family and...me. I was feeling a bit awkward about the whole thing. I'd met Elaine on several occasions, and we were certainly lightly acquainted with one another because I tried popping into events hosted by Corin and Wes whenever I was in town. But I wasn't that intimately connected to her that my presence here wouldn't raise an eyebrow or three. I was trying not to let myself think about that too deeply though because Rux had insisted on me being here, so...I was here.

Soon the party room was in fully swing until Wes signaled to the room that everyone should quiet down because his mom and dad were on the way. A few minutes passed before the doorbell sounded and all of us prepared to yell out "surprise!" as Penelope led her grandparents back to where everyone was all set up. She was the designated greeter because she was the least dressy of everyone who inhabited the house. While she'd put on a cute little a-line dress, it wasn't overtly "I've dressed to impress"...more "ugh, mom made me dress up for grandma and grandpa", meanwhile Wes and CoCo went full on formal—he in a tux and she in a ball gown. The party was had a lowkey Great Gatsby feel, with its opulence. Mrs. Elaine didn't seem too surprised when Pen led her and her husband back into the room, but no one but me seemed to notice. I think it's because I was the only person with no vested interest in pulling a fast one over on her that I could recognized the feigned emotions that played out on her face as everyone greeted her.

Rux had opted to wear a tux as well and looked entirely too damned appealing in it. He and Harlow had been making their rounds, greeting the folks gathered here tonight and catching up while like a creep, my eyes had tracked him around the room, taking in the ease with which he moved despite being such a massive dude. I wondered if that bigness extended all over. At the moment that thought crossed my mind, he looked in my direction, our eyes locking over the head of one of his mother's friends as he winked at me. I didn't even try to suppress the grin that minute action inspired, shaking my head. Harlow, who'd been propped on his waist leaned over to whisper something to him. They went back and forth a little before he placed her down onto her feet and she made her way over to me.

"Hey Miss Kai, I wanna come hang out with you since you don't have no friends here."

I laughed, taken aback at this blunt assessment of a damned toddler.

"Aw thanks, baby girl. I do have friends here, but they're

kinda busy celebrating your Lolly here. I'm just giving them the space to properly do that."

"Okay, well you're by yourself and I didn't like that. So, I told my daddy I was coming to talk to you. Do you know True?"

"I...uh...is True somebody here?" I asked, confused.

"No, silly," Harlow giggled, "She's on *Netflips...True and the Rainbow Kingdom.*"

My face must've definitely belied that I had no idea what she was talking about because Harlow launched into a detailed recap of who exactly this True character was...and all of her friends, plus the adventures on which they'd gone. I was a bit amazed as she managed to go on and on about this cartoon with impressive fortitude. She'd been going for a smooth ten minutes before her daddy waltzed up and told us both that it was time to sit down and get our grub on. Harlow protested until Rux told her we wouldn't be sitting far from one another. She grabbed my hand, leading me toward the table and when she realized that the place settings had me and her daddy on either side of her, squealed with delight. Rux and I shared a glance of amusement at Harlow's antics. I became even more impressed with his parenting skills when Harlow polished off all of her food without complaint of what was being served. Hell, some of the courses were things that were exactly my favorites, but Rux managed to keep her on task by reminding her of some sort of clean plate club deal they'd made in order for her to get dessert tonight.

Dessert, however, wasn't in little mama's plans because the excitement of the evening caught up to her before it was served. She straight up nodded off midsentence, which made me laugh as Rux explained that this was a recurring phenomenon. He left the party momentarily to get her settled into her room at *The Estate*, but no sooner than he'd left my side, the woman of the hour made her way to my side.

"Kai, right?" Mrs. Elaine said, approaching me with purpose.

"That's me," I choked out, nervously, "Ha-happy birthday, Mrs. Elaine."

"Oh honey, please call me Lane. No need to stand on formalities, we're damn near family after all, right?"

"I...uh..."

"Any friend of Corin's is definitely welcomed into the family. You know I just adore that girl," Mrs. Elaine...no, Mrs. *Lane* grinned, "I'm so glad you were able to join us tonight. This was quite the little shindig my kids put together, huh?" She leaned toward me a bit further and kept speaking in sotto voce, "We'll just keep it between us that I knew about it all along, right?"

I laughed along with her tinkling giggles, feeling somewhat validated that my hunch from earlier was absolutely correct.

"Absolutely," I said when I finally sobered, "after all CoCo and Wes worked so hard to pull everything off."

"And my Teddy, too. I'm sure you're familiar with his hard work as well?"

"I..."

"Hey, momtie, what you over here talking about?" Rux suddenly interrupted and I was thankful for the diversion.

I wasn't quite sure where that last little comment would lead us down the road of conversation since I couldn't quite get a read on Mrs. Lane.

"Boy, calm down. Nobody is telling any of your little secrets. I was just thanking Kai for attending my party is all."

"Mmmmhmmm," Rux replied suspiciously as Lane continued to giggle.

"I swear you're an old fuddy duddy like your uncle," she admonished.

"Aight woman, I'll show you fuddy duddy," Mr. Weston said, suddenly appearing over Mrs. Lane's left shoulder, "Come bring ya ass to the dance floor."

"Oh shit, here they go," Rux mumbled under his breath, with more mirth than anything lacing his tone.

Mr. Weston led Mrs. Lane onto the floor where they commenced to getting their entire life to Marvin Gaye's "Got to Give It Up" that the DJ was playing currently. Rux moved closer to me, lacing his arm around my waist and leaning down to speak directly into my ear, "C'mon, we can't let the fogies show us up, show me what you workin' with."

I let him lead me onto the floor as I teased, "Aight now, don't start none; won't be none."

Rux chuckled, "Did you turn sixty-five tonight, too, Kailene?"

"Hush," I said, falling into the groove of the uptempo hit, swaying my hips just enough to get Rux going, but not too much to cause a scandal.

Soon the floor was filled with everyone who attended the party getting their groove on as the DJ effortlessly slid from hit to hit, a playlist that had to be curated by Mr. Weston because every single song was one that made Mrs. Lane throw her hands in the air and yell out "hey, that's my *cut!*" We danced for the next couple of hours with intermittent breaks to have a drink or when someone who hadn't seen Rux in a while came over to chat with him. All in all, I had a great night with their family, celebrating the matriarch. I was ready to call it quits at just after midnight, having been up since before five am since my nervousness about seeing Rux in person for the first time had jolted me awake and I was unable to get back down. All of those nerves had been for naught because everything about this first meeting had gone nearly as perfect as perfect could get. No hiccups, no weird shit…just a great time had by the both of us as we crossed this bridge. I was just about to beg off when the DJ announced the last song of the night was about to be played.

As soon as the opening strains of the song began to play, I couldn't help the broad grin that stretched across my face. The song had long been one of my favorites, ever since I saw my mama and daddy dancing to it in the kitchen as a little girl. Rux, immediately sensing my pleasure at the selection, urged me back onto the dance floor, where we cut a mean two step to Stevie Wonder's "As". I leaned in close to Rux, reveling in his arms encapsulating me in a deep embrace as we moved.

He leaned down to speak into my ear, "Look at them. Still as smitten with each other as they've been since day one. This was their wedding song you know?"

"No kidding? This was my parents' first dance song as well."

I followed his gaze over to his aunt and uncle, seeing nothing but pure bliss on the face of the Moores as Mr. Weston crooned the words of the song directly into Mrs. Lane's ear.

"It's a classic, you can't go wrong with the greatest love song of all time."

"Facts."

The music wound down and Mrs. Elaine got on the microphone to thank everyone for coming out, as well as CoCo and Wes for hosting. I hung out for a bit as the crowd thinned, asking Co if she needed my help with the cleanup, but she assured me that she had a service coming in the morning and I should just chill. Despite having brought my bag to spend the night, a part of me wanted to head out and go home. That was quickly squashed by Corin as she reminded me of how much champagne I'd actually imbibed

NICOLE FALLS

this evening. Even though we were separated most of the night, I guess my good sis had been keeping tabs on me. She sent Rux to my car to retrieve my bag and put me up in a room that was closer to the quarters in which Rux and Harlow spent their time instead of my normal room near Penny. I knew exactly what she was doing, but there wasn't going to be any late-night creeping happening between Rux and I just yet. Despite us having been talking for nearly two months, my immense attraction and his willingness—I was just entirely too tired for anything to jump off. I didn't want the first time to be...lackluster. I wanted to be up, *alert* – an active participant in any sexual shenanigans that I'd partake in with Rux. And if the sleepy, lingering hug paired with a forehead kiss combo Rux left me at the threshold of my room's door with was any indication, he and I were on the exact same page.

The next morning, I woke up feeling...out of sorts. Entirely too early considering how late I'd gone down and I really wasn't interested in seeing much of anyone. I gathered my things, quietly, and tiptoed my ass past the room where I could clearly hear that Rux and his mini were still sawing logs and down the stairs on the way out of *The Estate*. I needed a moment or three to...decompress. I knew that this morning would be filled with commentary from CoCo and Wes, filled with sly innuendos toward Rux and I and...I just needed a *moment*. Last night was a good time, but the more I thought about it the more that the gathering we'd been at seemed to not be the perfect first time meet up shebang. And not that it needed to be perfect at all just... I sighed, not knowing what I needed but knowing it needed to not happen *here*. But of course as soon as I opened the massive front door of the house, Corin came jogging her ass right through it.

"Oh no ma'am...where do you think you're going?" she whisper-yelled.

"Home," I shrugged, continuing past her onto the garage where my car was stored.

"But...breakfast...and your boo...and..." she trailed off when she finally really looked at my face.

I guess whatever jumble of emotions that was currently swirling around in my brain was showing on my face because hers instantly transformed into a sympathetic moue.

"Oh honey," Corin cooed, "Go ahead, we'll see you later?"

I made a sound of inconclusive assent. I honestly didn't know. The only thing I did know was that my overwhelming need to be in my own house, laid out in my decompression room, surrounded by my Lovesac and doing deep restorative breathing exercises alongside the calming voice of the sis on the *What's Going Om?* app was highly necessary right now. My chest felt like an elephant was sitting on it and that big bitch Dumbo refused to raise up. I felt tears welling up, so with a quick embrace to Co, I hopped in my car and took off. No sooner than I hit the stop sign on the corner of their block, I felt the tears spilling down my cheeks and didn't even try to halt their progress. That tightness in my chest remained, even as I forced myself to inhale through my nose and exhale through my mouth. This attack had come out of nowhere, so sudden and swift that I finally just pulled off the road into the parking lot of a strip mall and let it work itself through. After about fifteen minutes or so, I finally felt calm enough to drive the rest of the way to my place to relax and unwind.

I pulled into my driveway and dragged myself out of the car, up the four steps leading to my townhome and beelined straight to my decompression room. Dedicating the small room that was supposed to be an office to becoming a little area of zen in my house mighta been the smartest idea I'd had in quite some time. Particularly in a moment like this where I couldn't readily identify what had triggered this attack. I eschewed the app, employing tricks I'd learned from a specialist we'd had at a *More to Life* retreat a few months ago. I also reached into the small refrigerator that I kept in the room and grabbed one of my self-prescribed anti-anxiety treats. As I laid there on the Lovesac, ascending to the point of it feeling like I was really laying in a cloud, I felt myself coming back to…close to normal. As such, I tried parceling out what exactly it was that had made me escalate to that former state of being. I mulled over the events of last night and quite frankly, there was nothing that had happened that would cause any adverse feelings to develop.

Hanging out at Elaine Moore's party had been a delight, honestly. Despite the nerves I had going in, I'd been fully embraced by that family in my…new sort of role, I guess. I hadn't known what to expect, really, going in. Corin assured me that I was getting in my head about everything. She'd been around them for enough years to be the expert, but…I couldn't wrap my head around it. I didn't know what I was expecting…actually—scratch that. I knew exactly what I was expecting to happen. I was expecting a repeat of a situation that I thought I'd completely moved past, but…apparently still haunted me.

I met Semaj in undergrad. I should have known he was a fuckboy based on that name alone. When I asked him about the genesis, he told me that his father's name was James and his mama wanted him to grow up to be the complete opposite of the kind of man his dad was so that's why she chose to name him the reversal of his name. I should have read that red flag immediately and cut off any sort of bonding with dude at the knees right there, but hindsight was twenty twenty for damn sure. We started off as friends, initially. We found ourselves in a lot of the same classes our first semester, he lived a floor below me in the dorms and we kinda just fell into an easy acquaintanceship. We went from politely speaking when we saw one another to exchanging contact information so that we could share notes when one or the other of us happened to miss a class we shared.

Our relationship was platonic for a few months before he asked me out. I was hesitant about it, but my roommate Amie, who was dating one of his friends at the time, assured me that he was a good dude that I should give a shot. Famous last words, to be honest. Semaj was charming as fuck, which was how I got swindled into being pulled into his web. Things between us progressed pretty quickly, bringing exclusivity and talks of spending the rest of our lives together into the picture after just a few months of dating. On the surface, he was exactly the kind of man that you wanted to bring home to your parents—just handsome enough, charismatic enough, intelligent enough to pass muster.

On the surface, all things were perfect between us. Everyone who saw us together swore we were perfectly suited, complementary and all of that, but my intuition told me that was something wasn't quite right with him about year into our courtship. I didn't recognize the signs of the emotional manipulation shit he pulled with me at first, honestly just caught up in the fact that I had someone who was so attuned to me that I ignored all of the gaslighting, lies, and shenanigans. Before Semaj my dating history was spotted at best, as I was sort of a later bloomer in the whole being attractive to the opposite sex department. It wasn't until, ironically enough, I took a human behavior course that I began to notice the clear signs of what I perceived to be nice or gentlemanly behavior was actually Semaj manipulating me to do his will and following his bidding despite what my own intuition was leading me to do.

I was torn between the feelings of immense satisfaction and belonging that I'd felt with him...and his family and friend groups, that I lost myself in our relationship completely. It wasn't until I was confronted with the harsh reality that for the entirety of our relationship, he had been dating multiple women and stringing them along with the same lies and fallacies he'd been selling me. The gag of it all was that his mother was privy to it all, having built varying levels of relationship with each of the four women he was juggling simultaneously. It was like they were playing some demented version of *The Bachelor*, not taking into account any of the detrimental effects that this sick game they were engaged in would have on any of us going forward. Last night, being surrounded by Rux's family, I now realized was a huge trigger, bringing back all of that mess with Semaj to the forefront. I'd been reeled in by the seemingly nice guy, with the stable family who wanted him to settle down with a good girl. Despite knowing logically that this situation was nothing like that shit I dealt with previously, I still felt over whelmed and confused. Was I rushing into this thing with Rux for the sake of having what I felt was a void in my life assuaged? Could I really trust that what was happening between us was real?

After a couple hours of staring into space and drifting off into a nap, I reawakened with...determination. I got up out of my decompression room and went in search of my phone. I just remembered it falling from my hand as I crossed the threshold of my front door. Hell, I'd hoped that I actually locked the front door when I came in this morning, honestly I had been moving on auto pilot, just trying to get to a place where I could come down from the heightened emotional state in which I'd left *The Estate*.

Walking into my living room I didn't see my phone on either of the small tables in there nor anywhere on the floor.

I kept going, down the hallway and toward the front foyer. It was nowhere to be found along that path either, which made me wonder had I even grabbed it from the charger in the room I stayed it last night or not. I really hoped that I had because the last thing I actually felt like doing was getting in my car and driving back across town to Corin and Wes'. It wasn't until I realized it was nowhere in my house that I got a little alarmed. I unlocked my front door, glad that I had at least had the presence of mind to do that and headed out toward my car. My eyes flitted along the sidewalk and grass, hoping to spot the bright red iPhone somewhere within the green and grey depths, but it wasn't there either. I let go a breath I hadn't realized I was holding when I looked inside my car and saw the phone nestled within a cupholder. I opened the door, sank down into the passenger seat and quickly retrieved it, ignoring the piles of alerts that littered the lock screen—navigating directly to the call screen. Hitting the name that was on the top of the list, I engaged a voice call, gnawing on my lower lip as the phone rang three times before the call was connected.

The call was barely engaged before I blurted, "Can you come? I need you." Willing those tears I felt welling back up in my eyes to stay at bay and not break through in my voice.

"Say less, I'm on the way. You need me to bring anything?"

I shook my head, not trusting my voice immediately, then cleared my throat. "No, just you."

TEN

"Whoa, where's the fire?" I said, damn near running into Corin as I made my way downstairs to get some much-needed coffee after last night.

"Sorry bro, just got a 911 from K...erm...I'm just in a rush is all," Corin pushed out on a harried breath, trying to get that lie past me like I didn't hear her begin to say a name that she shouldn't have had to say as said person was under this roof still.

I grabbed Corin by the elbow, halting her progress and pinning her with a stare, "Rinny."

"Teddy."

"What's going on with Kailene?"

"Wha—why you think something going on with friend? Huh?"

"She...isn't here, is she?" I sighed, running a hand over the top of my head.

"Ted—look, you trust me, right?"

"Implicitly."

"Then keep on trusting me. I'm trying not to lean on one

side of this more than the other because my loyalty lies with the both of you. But what I do need *you* to do is keep trusting me, okay?"

"Until you give me reason not to, I will."

"Fair enough, now can I...go? Promise to call you once I get this situation handled. I need you to promise me something though...don't get in your head about this, okay? Take the girls out, go visit Lane and Senior—do something, anything more than sit in this house thinking...no, *over-thinking* whatever is in your mind right now."

"Right now, I'm going to continue downstairs to make some coffee, that's all I've got in me for now."

"Again, fair enough, but I'm serious about what I said, Teddy."

I nodded, finished with the conversation for now. I wasn't a stupid man. I knew that Kailene had reservations about us...whatever this was we were doing currently, and I was at a loss for how to...reconcile that. All I knew was that I wanted her and thought those feelings were reciprocated. However, the look in her eyes when my Aunt Lane approached her last night with clear interrogation in her eyes, plus this little disappearing act this morning left me a bit less confident in that fact. As far as I knew, we were slow rolling into something that resembled a relationship.

I'd kept in constant communication with Kailene, revealing parts of myself that no other woman had been previously privy to. She and I talked in depth about issues that were important to the both of us, often getting into debates about some of the fundamental areas of conflict when it came to interpersonal conflicts. As someone who had his fair share of interaction with the fairer sex, I was convinced that I held the keys to knowing what made women tick, but Kailene turned my alleged knowledge on its ear every time. She challenged me with no hesitation, unafraid to make me defend some of the admittedly asinine opinions I'd long held onto. I wasn't quick to reveal this to her, but she definitely had a profound effect on the ways I saw couplings and relationships now, largely due to the fact that through conversations and reading her editorials, I'd grown fond of the woman I was slowly getting to know. She was very...deliberate in how she let her guard down with me, how much she truly let me in. I could tell that she was interested in the closeness that we were developing, but it also felt like she was holding back at times. I wasn't quite sure what the cause of the pullback was, but I was determined to break through whatever barriers were in place that would impede our eventual entrance into a monogamous relationship.

I honestly hadn't known what to expect or what I'd expected when I answered her ad, but the more I learned about Kailene, but more I wanted her to be *mine*. I'd sweated both Wes and Rinny for additional details about her dating history, dudes she'd messed with before me...anything that would give me some insight into the parts of her she'd deftly dodged questions about. Granted, I had given her the cliff's notes version of how things had gone down with women in my life prior to her arrival in it. She knew that I'd been a little bit of a manwhore, but not exactly the depths of that manwhorism. That also required me to give her the whole story about how things went down with Britton and Harlow's eventual conception. That was something I was still working through myself, honestly and didn't know how to broach with a woman to whom I was trying to show the "new" me. Honestly, maybe it was best that she took leave now before either one of us got hurt, eventually.

"Man, why are you sitting here looking like somebody just told you that big boys are outta style, fam?" Wes joked, coming to sit down at the table with me.

"Man, get outta here," I laughed, waving him off, "the

ladies will forever love a teddy bear typa brotha such as myself. Don't be mad that only one lady ever wanted to give your kindling looking ass a shot. You should be worshipping the very ground that Rinny walks on before a strong gust of wind comes along and blows your twig ass away, g."

"Bruh, let's not act like I wasn't beating 'em off with this stick in my day," Wes shot back.

"Uncle Wes you beat people with sticks?" a surprised Harlow whisper yelled as she and Penelope walked into the room.

I groaned, throwing a hand over my face. I swear this little girl and her supersonic hearing was going to be the death of any adult trying to have civilized conversation in a thirty-mile radius.

"Harlow Marie…was Uncle Wes talking to you?"

"I…" she trailed off, at least having the decency to look somewhat contrite, "sorry for *eve's droppin'*, daddy."

"Don't be sorry, LowLow, be careful," Pen whispered.

I stifled a laugh before I asked Pen to repeat herself. Penelope mumbled some nonsense under her breath. Those two were thick as thieves and identical in behavior, barely knowing how to maintain a child's place as their overzealous and curious natures led most often to them getting checked about minding the business that minds them as opposed to hopping headfirst into adult business. I'd consistently asked Aunt Lane how to curb that instinct, but she was quick to remind me and Wes both that the girls' inclination was inherited honestly. I'd liked to think that my curiosity had been well kept, but Aunt Lane burst that bubble immediately, reminding me of the many times that she'd boxed both mine and Weston Junior's ears for perking up when they should have laid dormant.

Penelope quickly changed the subject, lamenting that she and Harlow were both dying from hunger and the only cure was Uncle Rux's special waffles. The girls were lucky that I was in a vulnerable state right now, unable to resist the twin pleading pouts that graced their faces as I gathered the ingredients to appease their appetites. Wes joined me in cooking, frying up some bacon and scrambling eggs to accompany the waffles. Just as we'd finished up and sat down to eat, my phone rang and I jumped up to grab it, thinking it was Corin checking in with me. Instead it was a FaceTime request from Britton. I swiped to engage the phone call and propped it up in front of Harlow who had a mouthful of waffles as she greeted her mother. Britt and I chastised her in unison to swallow then speak before I checked out of their conversation and tucked into my own plate.

After breakfast, Penelope and Harlow disappeared to Pen's room while Wes and I cleaned up the kitchen the retreated to his den to watch some football. Our team had a bye this week, but that didn't stop us from get entirely too emotionally involved in the games broadcast this week and placing a few wagers. We couldn't resist the pull of competition, that natural brotherly inclination of trying to one up each other while flexing our knowledge of the sport. I'd played football throughout high school, but gave it up in undergrad choosing an academic scholarship instead, while Wes had never quite been physically coordinated enough to play any sport, but analytical enough that he could read the field and call plays in ways that not even I, with my intimate knowledge of playing the sport, could. Watching the games had distracted me from the fact that it'd been hours since Corin had left the house on her urgent errand and I hadn't heard a peep from her since.

My patience was at an all-time low and I picked up my phone to reach out just as my text tone went off. I picked it up just to see an address. The text came from Corin, so I'd assumed that this was Kailene's home address. There were no directions or anything additional, just the address. I texted back with a series of question marks and all I received in return was the cryptic message that the door was open and to come over with my mind in the same state—*open*. I asked Wes to continue to keep an eye on Harlow and was met with a derisive snort as if I'd insulted him.

"Man, if you don't get outta here and gone and spend some quality time with your lady. Low Low is always welcomed around these parts, bro."

"Man, the jury's still out about that *my lady* part, but thanks bro, appreciate you," I replied, dapping him up before running upstairs to quickly change and make my way over to Kailene's.

When I arrived, I was met at the front door by Corin who immediately shushed me with a finger over her lips and halted my entrance into the house.

"Okay, so I should tell you that I didn't exactly tell her that you were coming over," Corin whispered.

"Rinny!" I exclaimed, throwing my hands up in exasperation, "are you on my side here or not?"

"Theodore Warren Reed. Relax. I know what I'm doing here. And I need you to listen to me *carefully*. I need you to enter this house with an open mind and listening ear. My sister is in a really vulnerable place right now and I need you to handle her gingerly."

"I...what does that mean, Rin? You keep speaking in riddles."

"Because it's not my business to tell, but...let me ask you this? How much have you told her about you and Britton?"

"Why is that important?"

"So...not much if you answering my question with a question is any indication. Okay. Hm. Y'all need to talk, Teddy. Like...no more of this skirting around anything. A real life laying the cards on the table, baring it all kind of talk. I...stay right here."

Before I could even reply, Corin disappeared back into the house, not fully closing the door, and I could hear her talking to Kailene in a low, soothing tone before I heard Kailene's voice raise briefly. I couldn't make out the details of the conversation and was half a second from just barging into the house when Corin reappeared and shooed me into the house. With a pat on the shoulder, and a "good luck bro", she jogged out of the house, and down the stairs into her car. I ventured further into the house, just to the living room but Kailene was nowhere in sight. Not wanting to alarm her I called out.

"Kailene, hello?"

"Upstairs...I'll be down in a minute," she called back, her voice sounding muffled, almost clogged, "You can sit down in the living room."

I did as suggested, settling in on her loveseat and tuning the television over to CBS while I waited for her return. I wasn't quite sure what I'd walked into and could at least use the distraction of football until she reappeared. I sucked in a breath because she looked beautiful as usual, pretty brown skin glowing as a smile that did not reach her eyes graced her full mouth. Her eyes were a bit glossy, nose slightly tinged red as if she'd been crying. I stood immediately, crossing the room in a couple steps to wrap her in my embrace. She inhaled, a shuddering sort of breath before squeezing me a bit tighter and then pulling back to look up at me.

"Hey," she exhaled softly, then dropped her gaze as she tried to withdraw from my hold.

I halted that progress, keeping her close to me until the cadence at which our hearts beat was in synchronicity. Then I led her over to the loveseat, still keeping her close but allowing our hold to be slightly broken as I gazed down upon her. We sat in silence for a minute or so as I saw her mentally calculating what she wanted to say when she eventually spoke. She opened her mouth a few times as if she'd finally gathered her thoughts, but they never quite made it from her brain to cross her lips.

"Can I just say something?" I asked softly, bringing her gaze to entangle with mine once again as she nodded.

"I'm scared as shit right now. Stomach knotted on the verge of the bubble guts because I have no idea what is going on in your mind right now and that's fucking with me. I ain't never had a woman have me this...*shook*. I'm not used to being on this side of the breakup so...just let me down easy aight?"

"Rux, I..."

"Nah, I'm for real sweetheart. If I ain't what you thought I would be, I'm cool with you just being honest about it now and we can move forward like all the rest never happened. I wouldn't want things to be awkward out at *The Estate* or whatever so..."

"Rux!" Kailene broke into my little impromptu speech I'd freestyled, "I'm not breaking up with you. First off, we haven't even declared what it is that we're doing here, exactly so I kinda can't break up with you. And...beyond all of that, so far you are exactly as advertised which...has *me* a little...*shook* as you put it. This weekend wasn't supposed to go like this, at all. We were supposed to finally meet in person, hang out with your fam, and then I was going to bring you back here and fuck your brains out. I mean after all, wasn't all of this corresponding and calling and texting we were doing just mental foreplay meant to ultimately culminate in one or the other of us calling bluffs and tumbling headfirst into my bed, making good on those promises made in late night phone sessions? See if the hype that had been built up on both sides was more than simply that?"

I said nothing, but my mouth had dropped open and remained there after the phrase "fuck your brains out" had spilled from Kailene's lips. We'd been gingerly dancing around acting on the obvious physical attraction crackling between the two of us. Of course I had wanted to carry her off and have my way with her the instant she appeared behind me in that mirror out at *The Estate*. I'd seen more than my fairshare of pictures of Kailene thanks to her propensity for selfies, but also Getty Images capturing her at the many events she'd attended over the years. That day at *The Estate*, however, she looked downright edible—dressed simply in a long, bright red dress that highlighted the subtle curves of her mostly lithe frame. But the look of trepidation I'd seen in her eyes when we were finally face to face allowed my good sense to override my baser instincts. Another thing that was...different for me. In the past I'd had no problem ignoring any warning signs or flags in pursuit of hedonistic pleasure. But something about Kailene had me eschewing all of my normal ways and habits to ensure her comfort.

"You know what you never asked me? In all of these weeks of communicating? You've never asked me why I placed that ad in the first place. And I never asked you why you responded. Because I didn't want to get into any of the... complicated histories and previous circumstances that led us both to meeting in the place that we currently sit. But, CoCo, my good sis sat here and reminded me of just how foolish I was to expect that we wouldn't have to delve deeper, have these more difficult conversations about what our expectations and standards were. Like we wouldn't need to clearly define boundaries and just exactly what we were doing here. Instead I was content to blur lines from the very beginning.

Letting myself get close to you and attached to Harlow...

your baby girl...so soon without even knowing what the hell her daddy and I were getting ourselves into. What we were unwittingly bringing *her* into. And I woke up this morning with all of these thoughts and plenty others revolving around my past relationship sins and the signs I consistently ignored rushing through my brain. And it was *a lot. Overwhelmingly so*. So, I took to the familiar and got myself out of there. *Quickly*. Because I thought space would give me the answers I sought. Instead it brought more questions. And instead of calling the one person who could answer any of those questions, I instead burrowed deeper into myself. Sending myself through a whirlwind of mess in the past few hours."

Kailene had broken eye contact with me less than a quarter of the way through this...unloading. She kept speaking, knowing I was there, but not giving my presence intense attention. I let her get it all out, not wanting to interrupt as she went into deeper detail about her reasoning behind the personal ad. As I listened to her detail how her life was perfect to her until she was hit with this burning desire to have someone to share it with, I found myself *now* being able to relate to this sudden feeling of...*needing* companionship. But not just with anyone, with Kailene, specifically. It was what led to me replying to Kailene's ad and continuing with this pen pal courtship weirdness and getting to know her better despite our lives being entirely too entangled if things happened to not work out for us in the romantic sense. I just wanted *her*.

"I just...this all is too much, too quickly. And I've been here before, falsely lulled into thinking something was one way and it turned out to be another. I can't be that girl again. *I refuse to be that girl again*. So, what I'm saying is that we should probably cut our losses and just pull back from this now. Before we ruin everything. There's too much at stake here, Rux…and I just…that is basically the conclusion I've come to," Kailene said with finality.

"So, you *are* breaking up with me?" I asked, dumbfounded.

"You can't break up with someone you aren't…" she started but I cut in.

"Sweetheart, if you think I lay up on the phone with a woman at all hours of the day and night because I want to be available whenever her schedule allows me the time? If you think I'm introducing my daughter who is my literal heart roaming this world outside of my body to just anybody? If you think I've ever sweated my bro and sis about the most miniscule of details about any woman who I didn't think of as mine? Sweetheart, you are gravely mistaken. This ain't a game for me. No flight by night shit, a diversion to pass the time. We've been skating around the issue for the same reason if your little soliloquy is any indication—we're both two punk ass individuals afraid of giving into feelings that we weren't a hundred percent certain were reciprocated despite our actions confirming what we knew deep down. And we can try to justify things to ourselves as much as we'd like to, but the fact of the matter is that we've been building something solid this whole time, Kailene.

It's what made you too nervous to show up to breakfast yesterday, it's what had me in the barber shop getting a line up despite having just gotten my hair cut by my barber two days before. It's what led you running from *The Estate* this morning and what's had me sitting around with a tight bootyhole all morning as I waited on Rinny to tell me something…*anything* about what was going on with you and how or if I'd somehow managed to fuck this all up. But one thing I want to be evidently clear is that I care about you, Kailene. *A lot*. More than you are probably ready to hear or that I'm ready to express at this moment but fuck it. This is something completely foreign to me, but I'm all in."

I grabbed her hands, encasing them with mine as I squeezed and repeated that last line, "I'm all in, sweetheart. Good, bad, ugly, indifferent. And I'm probably gonna fuck up...a lot...but I hope you don't give up on me. I need you to *not* give up on me."

"Can...I ask you something? You don't have to answer if you don't want to, but I...it's something I need to know..." Kailene trailed off, breaking our eye contact briefly before meeting my gaze once more, "Why didn't things work out with you and Harlow's mom?"

I drew in a sharp breath, exhaling harshly. I didn't want to answer this because I knew that I ran the risk of running Kailene off with the truth, but I also knew that she deserved nothing less than the truth if we were going to move forward. And if I was being completely honest with myself, I needed to own my culpability in how things went down with Britton.

"So...Britton and I weren't exactly...officially together ever."

"When you say *officially together* you mean...?" Kailene prodded.

"In any sort of official relationship. I've never really done the relationship thing with *any woman*, if I'm keeping it a buck. I've always kept women around, but never in any official girlfriend capacity. We kicked it, chilled, went out to eat, fucked, all that. But never really put any names on what we were to each other. And let me be clear, that went both ways. If at any time any woman I was kicking it with felt like she didn't like our arrangement she could feel free to disengage, no harm no foul."

The grimace on Kailene's face at that statement almost

made me regret the level of honesty I'd begun this explanation with, but it was too late to turn back now.

"So, you were the fuckboy prototype?" she mumbled, pulling back to cross her arms over her chest as I continued.

"In hindsight, yes? In the thick of it, however, I thought I was…clear and upfront. However, I found myself giving women the impression that things between us were one way when they were another. Britton was one of those women who believed that she would be the one to change me, that somehow our connection was deeper than the one I'd shared with any women who came before her and she'd be the one to make me see the light. The words that came out of my mouth consistently contradicted my actions when it came to Britton. So, we had been doing our thing for a few years when she hinted at wanting us to put some parameters on what we had going. She intimated that she was ready to settle down and have some kids but that wasn't on my radar at that point in time at all. Now this part I'm not exactly proud of, but I doubled down on insisting that she knew what we had was and that if she thought that her pussy was enough to change that then she had the world completely fucked up. As far as I knew that was the final straw for her and she fell back. I kept on doing my thing out in the world and that was that. Until one day I literally ran into Britton and she was accompanied by evidence of our time together that she couldn't quite deny—Harlow."

Kailene gasped, "Wait, she kept your baby from you?"

I nodded, "Apparently when she was doing all of that hinting about me settling, she'd just learned that she was pregnant. Instead of telling me outright, she just kept dropping hints that I had no interest in retrieving. Once she finally figured that out, she bounced on me. Convinced that she was doing the best for herself and her unborn child. I took one look at Harlow and knew she was mine."

"Well yeah, she literally stole your face," Kailene laughed.

"Facts," I chuckled right along with her before quickly sobering, "but...well, here is the part where we kinda...no, *I definitely* fucked up. We went to court, got all the DNA testing and shit out of the way, the formal declaration that Harlow was my kid and I backslid. It began with Britt not wanting Harlow to come stay by me without her presence and me being acquiescent because she definitely knew our daughter better than I did. We hung out a lot as a family in the very beginning, wanting Harlow to get acclimated to having both a mommy and daddy in her life now. But...in all of that hanging out, Britt and I kinda blurred the lines between co-parents and lovers, slipping back into our old comfortable roles.

You know, I grew up with my aunt and uncle—Wes' parents? The example they set was something that had always been in the back of my mind, so knowing that Britton was out here in this world with my seed had me thinking that she and I needed to get past whatever differences we had and get together to make it work for our kid, right? She deserved to not come from a broken home. I knew that Britt and I weren't really compatible to be more than friends, but I needed my baby girl to have that Huxtable upbringing that I'd been fortunate enough to have once I went to live with my Aunt Lane and Uncle Weston. She didn't need mommy over here dating whoever and daddy doing his thing only popping in here and there. That happy family shit was short-lived and eventually I realized that the only good thing to come from Britton and I's coupling *was* Harlow."

Kailene drew in a breath, "*Ouch.*"

"As you can well guess, that did not go over well with Britton who, might I add, was in a relationship with someone when I pitched this whole idea of she and I trying to get together for the sake of Harlow."

"Jesus, Rux."

"I know...not...one of my finer moments. And Britton definitely has not let me forget it with the contentious energy that remains between us to this day. I know...this is a lot, too much for you to take in, but I couldn't not be completely honest with you about everything and how it shook out, Kailene. I couldn't enter into anything with you, without you knowing the whole truth of my situation with Britt and you making a decision about how you want us to proceed based on all of that. I know it's kind of unfair of me to lay that all on you at once and then force your hand to make a decision, so I'ma give you some time to absorb all of that before you let me know how you want to proceed, sweetheart. But I need you to know that all of that fuckboy behavior is done for on this end."

"*Allegedly.*"

I had to eat that because as far as she knew *now*, I was a Fuckboy Supreme. Kailene had no reason to believe I had completely rehabilitated and was rid of that energy that previously drove my life. All of the words in the world from me or anyone else wouldn't be able to convince her of that after what I'd just shared, I was sure.

"I..."

"How can I be sure...certain that after two, three months you won't be giving me the same speech you'd given to all of the ones who came before me. You just laid out an entire field of red flags in front of me, honestly, Rux. You are the exact type of man who was the reason for me starting *More to Life*...and I'm supposed to ignore all of that based on what exactly?"

I cleared my throat, trying to rid it of the lump that suddenly appeared in it, "That's fair, you're completely right, Kailene. Hell, if the shoe was on the other foot, I wouldn't know how to receive any of this either. But...is my complete transparency not an indication of my seriousness here?"

"Or is it a way for me to let my guard down, so I can let you in only to be disappointed? This is...too much right now. Can you just...I need..." she trailed off, shaking her head.

I read the room, catching the vibe. She needed space— some time to figure out just how she wanted to proceed forward if at all. I didn't like it, but I didn't have much of a choice of whether or not I liked it, I had to accept it. Kailene was well within her rights to completely let this go, let us go...move forward and find someone in whom she could place her complete trust instead of being precariously balanced, waiting for the bottom to fall out. No matter how much I wanted her, needed her presence in my life, the karmic retribution of the way I'd treated every single woman who'd led me to her was finally coming home to roost. And I had no one to blame for the shit, but myself. I rose up from the loveseat and Kailene did the same, almost robotically unaware of her action. I pulled her in for a brief embrace, placing a lingering kiss on her forehead.

"Whenever you make your decision, you know how to reach me," I whispered into her ear before taking my leave.

I left Kailene's house feeling out of sorts and not exactly ready to face my mega-intuitive little girl who'd have a million and one questions about what was going on with her daddy, so instead I just let my subconscious lead me to where I knew I'd eventually end up. As I pulled my car to a stop in front of the curb of my childhood home, a rueful grin crossed my lips. Uncle Weston was outside raking up the mess of leaves left by the large Ash trees that flanked both sides of the yard. Aunt Lane sat on the porch swing on the large, wraparound porch pretending not to be overseeing his process, but we all knew she was paying keen attention to whatever he was doing and not the book that rested upon her lap as she called out to Uncle Weston.

"Look who had the nerve to come over here without my dumplin'!" Aunt Lane called out jovially, directing Uncle Wes' attention to me as I drug myself from the car toward the house.

The sluggishness in my gait quickly halted further teasing from Uncle Wes as he observed my demeanor.

"Me or Lane?" he asked simply when I was close enough for him to see the painful look I was sure had been permanently etched onto my features since I'd left Kailene's.

I nodded toward my aunt, "Her first, but you, too."

"Aight, youngblood, we'll rap," he said, turning back to his task at hand.

As soon as I stepped the first foot on the stairs, Aunt Lane took one look at me and rushed forward enveloping me in a hug. Her embrace was all it took for me to completely break down, "I messed up, auntie. I messed up real bad."

"Aw, baby, let's go inside," Aunt Lane said with a firm hand at my back, escorting me into the house to settle in her office.

As we settled on her couch, I ran down what had gone down with Kailene as Aunt Lane quietly listened, letting me get all of my feelings out without interjection which was rare for her. One thing I had always loved about growing up with my aunt and uncle was their willingness to always have conversations about our feelings with us. It was something that I didn't realize was out of the norm until I was in the early years of my undergraduate career. Aunt Lane normally would break in with clarifying questions if she thought I was seeking advice, but today she just let me completely unload. And when I was done, eyes wet with unshed tears she asked one thing.

"Baby...you're in love with this girl, aren't you?"

I inhaled sharply, not wanting to answer the question because it seemed impossible. In the past, feelings for a woman didn't develop that quickly with me, no matter how much constant communication and positive energy flowed between the two of us. But on brand for the completely foreign initiation and progression of this connection with Kailene were these intensely strong emotions I already felt for her. I was still hesitant to call it love, as that was an emotion that, in a romantic sense, was wholly unfamiliar for me to be able to adequately pinpoint. My silence, however, communicated what my mouth refused to say in response to my aunt's question which just prompted her to keep speaking.

"I know this is the last thing that you want to hear, but you've got to let it run its course, baby. If this is the real thing, you and Kailene will find your way back to one another sooner or later, but you just have to be patient, let things roll out how they're going to go down. The universe never lets true love stray too far for too long. But if this wasn't in the divine's plans for you all then," she trailed off shrugging, "You just need to remain secure in your feelings, son."

"But what if my feelings are wrong? If I'm sitting out here on a limb by myself."

"Believe me baby, after witnessing the two of you in a room together, even from afar? You ain't out here on your own. Just give it time to work through."

I nodded in assent, spent from trying to argue against a woman who wouldn't back down from a position she believed to be *the position*. Instead I went to find my uncle, seeking the male perspective on this whole situation. Running everything down for what I knew wouldn't be the last time today, Uncle Wes' reply surprised the hell out of me. He was on that whole universe bringing true love together by any means necessary math that Aunt Lane was on. He wasn't really a *woo woo energies and vibes* sort of dude, way too old school to give into any newfangled ideas of reading individuals, so I was a little shook by his advice. The both of them doubling down cemented the idea of not pressuring Kailene and waiting on the anointed time for us to reunite.

ELEVEN

KAI

"**B**oss lady, you good?" Arelia asked, bringing me back to the present, where we sat in our normal Monday morning staff meeting and all attention was on me.

"My bad, y'all, I zoned for a minute," I said, shaking my head and refocusing my attention, "where were we?"

"Just wrapped up the final details of the Winter *More to Life* Weekend. Jes confirmed that we were able to get the ladies of *MYOP* to agree to do the Saturday afternoon session and *NoahKnows* for Sunday's keynote address. We were just wondering if there were any additional loose ends that we'd somehow forgotten to follow up with you about?"

I looked down at the list of items that I'd had questions about, my notes from their presentations earlier in the meeting showing that everything that I was worried about for this even had already been handled by them. I shouldn't have been surprised, honestly, as my team was hand curated to be able to function in my absence and they continually showed me that they could do what I needed them to do and more. Despite me being more physically present in the home office, I was definitely just here in body and not really mind and spirit in the past few weeks. It'd been almost three weeks since things went...not *south* exactly but on pause between Rux and me. He'd laid some pretty heavy information on me and I'd been processing it...weighing my options about the risks versus rewards. And Corin, in her infinite wisdom, was of zero help. She told me that she would be staying out of it, when she and I talked after he left my house and...that wench had the nerve to actually stick to her word.

Normally she *couldn't wait* to offer her opinion on moves I should make—from the most miniscule to major life decisions, but the one time I needed her to weigh in she remained mum. Even Wes aka mouth almighty had nothing to say after I'd cornered him at a park, I knew he liked to run in twice a week in the early hours of the morning. After I'd suitably scared the shit outta him by rolling up on him, he echoed the words of his wife that this was a decision I'd have to make on my own because neither of them wanted culpability if the result was not favorable for me. I respected them sticking to their guns, but also really wished someone would just tell me what to do.

The only thing I did know for sure was that not talking to Rux over these past few weeks had left quite a chasmic void in my daily life, which should have been answer enough, but I still didn't trust it. My gut had led me astray before when I put my all of trust into Semaj, and quite frankly I didn't trust the bitch when it came to men in which I held some sort of interest, at all. Business decisions? My gut was sound. Sussing out someone else's man and his bullshit? It was even more sound. When it came to putting myself on the line and possibly getting my heart broken though? My gut was zero for three and I wasn't chomping at the bit to increase the number in the loss column any time soon. The fact was Rux was a walking, talking red flag based on the history that he'd run down to me about his relationship or lack thereof with Harlow's mama. His saving grace and the only thing that still had me questioning if my decision to cut us off at the pass was the contrition I heard in his tone as he detailed how he was done with his former fuckboy behavior. It rang sincere to me, honestly. I wanted to believe him, needed to believe him, and my gut...she was on Team Rux. My rational brain however, was still on the fence.

I shook my head again, clearing all thoughts of Rux and tuning back into the meeting enough to close it out and give out assignments for our next check-in. As I adjourned the meeting, I noticed Arelia peering at me with an unreadable expression on her face. As the room emptied and it was just she and I left, she lagged a bit before seemingly coming to a decision in her own mind and speaking up.

"Are you sure you're okay, boss lady? You've been..." she stopped, seeming to consider the next words that would drop from her mouth, "a little fuzzy around the edges lately."

The word edges instantly made me thrust a hand upward toward my hairline, causing Arelia to giggle a bit.

"I didn't mean your literal edges, boss lady. Those are laid and slayed per usual...you just seem...out of focus a bit. I don't want to overstep, but everyone's pretty concerned and I was nominated as tribute to say something in the *Slack* channel that we created to discuss you privately."

"Y'all created a new *Slack* channel? Damn," I giggled, "I'm...it's been that bad?"

"You were literally in a catatonic state in for three-quarters of this meeting, Kai. Yeah, it's been that bad. I know we're just boss and subordinate, but I'd like to think that since I'm one of few who have been here since the beginning that we're friends of sorts too? Not super close because you like to keep your circle small, but in case you need like...an unbiased opinion or sounding board, I want you to know that I'm here. For you. If that's what you need. And if not, then I'm sorry for overstepping."

"I...thank you, Arelia. I'll take that into consideration. Hey, I'm gonna take off for the day. So y'all can openly discuss my weird behavior instead of being resigned to *Slack*," I winked, with a halfhearted giggle.

With that I walked out of the conference room to my office to gather my things and sent a quick message to the group chat asking Corin and Tina to meet at my place at their earliest convenience. I needed my girls to keep it real with me and in order for that to happen I had to make sure that the both of them were nice and loose. On the way to my house, I stopped off at the local liquor store to grab a few bottles of wine to accompany the half bottle of wine I had left at the house. I'd order in some terrible snacks and we were all set to have a total hen party. Surprisingly, Tina was the first one to hit me back, letting me know that she was game to give work the "something bad happened" excuse and duck out immediately. Corin tagged in a few minutes later as I was checking out in the store. She was ready to come over as well. Both asked if they needed to bring anything with them, but I assured that their presence was good enough. We settled on a meeting time of a half an hour from now in order to give me time to get home and settled before they wandered in.

By the time the both of them showed up, I was back in what had become my customary attire around the house these days—black leggings, an oversized grey crewneck that exposed my left shoulder and my grey and white striped fuzzy foot socks. CoCo always teased me about the redundancy of calling these specific socks my "foot socks" as if there were other parts of the body to be socked.

"Oh shit, CoCo, she brought out the nice, stemless glasses for us and not those plastic joints she normally tries to get us to drink out of ever since you broke her *Waterford* glass," Tina crowed as they came into the house.

"Celestine, I really wish you'd stop trying to pin your crime on me, baby girl. Everyone knows you're clumsier than a newborn baby deer," Corin joked back, coming straight to embrace me and press a quick kiss against my cheek, "Hey, baby. You good?"

I nodded, quickly moving to give Tina a quick hug before settling back in my chair, with my feet tucked beneath my bottom and clutching my oversized glass which was filled nearly to the brim with the half bottle of wine I'd been making my way through this week. I'd put out a decent little spread of cheese, crackers, sausage, and fruit to accompany our wine. Both of the ladies poured themselves generous servings of wine, settled into their normal posts in my living room and then proceeded to stare a hole through me.

"What?" I asked.

They looked at each other, smirking, as if trying to decide which of them was going to speak first, then back at me.

"You called this little tribunal council, cousin...so spill..." Tina finally said as we sat there in a few moments of silence.

I knew she would be the first one to crack, she never could stand moments like this...intense silence, the air crackling with unspoken words.

"I...think I've made a decision," I started, slowly.

"About?" Tina further prodded.

"Rux."

Neither of them said anything, Corin sucked in a sharp breath. I was honestly shocked too because as far as I knew, up until that moment I hadn't made a decision. I was still vacillating between down which path to travel and that was why I'd called them over here in the first place. But when they sat down and I looked over to the large whiteboard that I'd dragged down from my office for them to help me make a pro/con list, the feeling of knowing exactly what I needed to do washed over me as if I hadn't been grappling with my decision all this time.

"What? Cat got your tongue?" I giggled.

"Well, I thought that one was persona non grata around here. Verboten. Candyman. He whose name shant be spoken. Voldemort." Corin finally spoke up.

"I've been that bad?"

"The last time I accidentally mentioned him in passing you didn't talk to me for three days," Tina said.

"That's not true, I've been busy with tying up loose ends for the *MTL* weekend."

"Your team has all that shit on lock, you straight up blocked me. I know you did because when I called you from Mama's phone it went straight through to ringing even though you didn't pick up. Whenever I'd called from my phone during that same timeframe it went straight to voice-mail. But I knew you were on your Brandy and Wanya shit, so I let you have it. But know, I don't appreciate that shit, sister-cousin. Straight up."

"Awwww, I'm sorry, baby," I said, getting up from my perch in my comfy recliner and dropping down alongside her on the loveseat to snuggle up close to her.

"Mmmhmm, whateva heffa. So, what's your decision? You ready to give one of these other guys a fair shot?" Tina asked, leaning forward to pick at the small pile of additional interested bachelors who'd tried shooting their shot over the past few weeks.

Men who, if I were being perfectly honest with myself, weren't worth the ink on a postcard length reply. I knew who I wanted. I knew what I wanted. And I'd kept the both of us in misery for long enough while I pretended that this could go any other way. I wanted to see where things would go with Rux. The connection that we'd forged in such a short period of time was undeniable and I'd go the rest of my life wondering what if, if I didn't at least give myself a shot at seeing what this new and improved him was like. The ugliness of the man he'd described with Britton wasn't ever shown to me while he and I were in the beginning stages of trying to build our...whatever. And it could have just been smoke and mirrors or a very good acting job on his behalf, but my gut...my treacherous ass, barely to be believed gut told me that it wasn't. That he was sincere and could possibly be what I'd been looking for since I started this quest to find...*my guy.*

"So...y'all got any tips how to get a man back or nah?"

Both Tina and Corin jumped up cheering. "Thank God you made the right choice," Corin crowed, "I didn't want to have to disown you sis, but we were close."

"Coco," Tina gasped on a giggle.

"Really, Co?" I asked, incredulously.

"Absolutely. I love you, Kai. God knows I do, but Teddy is my heart. I've known that boy and loved that boy for as long as I've known and loved my husband. And I've always known that his manwhore antics were a coverup for deeper hurt that he'd never quite worked through. I mean damn, imagine losing your mother at a young age, never knowing your father, being uprooted from the only environment you'd previously known and having to readjust and adapt to coming into the goddamn Huxtables. Because let's face it, sis, that's what the Moores are. Cliff and Clair of Belleview. Shit, even I was shook when Weston took me to meet them for the first time. If you're not used to that kind of environment, it can take a lot of adjustment. And from the little Teddy has shared with me about what he remembers of life with his mom before she passed? Yeah...it was definitely a shock to the system coming here. So needless to say, I've always had a soft spot for him—something that

133

drives Wes batty to this day. I've witnessed Teddy's growth though Kai and honestly would not have encouraged you to pursue anything with him if I thought he was less than sincere."

"Ok so where was all of this when I asked you what I should do three weeks ago?" I pouted.

"Girl, you weren't in the headspace to hear any of this. You were reeling from that intense bout of honestly that he'd hit you with and anything I would have argued upon his behalf would have fallen on deaf ears. You were dead set on having been deceived and logic had no place in your life at that point?"

"And in the weeks following?"

"You needed to come to whatever conclusion you were going to on your own, Kai. It wasn't my place...or Tina's place... or your mama's place...to try to dissuade you of whatever you needed to work through in order to finally reach a decision that would make you happiest. I know you like our input, baby...and we relish that you hold us in such high regard, however, we couldn't make this decision for you. We weren't privy to the innermost recesses of your mind, the depth of the connection that you and he made... none of that. Nobody but the two of you had the power to determine how things would progress forward."

"Okay Dr. Philisha," Tina cracked.

I giggled along with the two of them but sobered quickly.

"I was serious though, about needing advice on how to get a man back. You know...this is all new territory to me. I've never gone ghost hunting."

That set the two of them off laughing again. I'd contended over and over that all of my exes were resting in perfect peace. There was no need to go in reverse once I was done with a situation, so sorry to those men. Rux was actually the first and only to make me reconsider remembering that he actually existed on this mortal plane. Another fact that made me giving him another shot a foregone conclusion, honestly.

"I honestly don't think you'll have to do too much if that hangdog, bedraggled puppy look of his that I've seen every time he and Pen or Wes are on FaceTime is any indication," Corin tutted, "Whew, my brother has been going through. And it's been killing him not to ask me anything about you, I can just tell."

"Girl, the man was on Instagram Carl Thomasing the other night. Instasnap after instasnap of the saddest love songs imaginable talmbout he was just vibing while burning some midnight oil," Tina piped up, "I was just waiting on the Lenny Williams to come out, but he must've regained a bit of his dignity before he went there."

"Nah," Corin popped in giggling, "Wes clowned him so much about being emo in front of company that he went back and deleted the whole story, Tee. Because my man definitely hit those 'ohs' that Uncle Lenny sang loud and proud for the world to hear."

"Nooooo," Tina groaned, "Damn, you hate to see a player go out like that."

"I didn't know you followed him on IG, Tee," I said. I'd recently blocked Rux on all forms of social media while I took my time trying to figure out what the future between the two of us would look like, so I wasn't privy to any of what she was talking about.

"It's super recent, actually...after he...started following me. I'm sure it was just because he was hoping to catch a glimpse of you in my stories, sis. Before IG got rid of the explore tab, I noticed that he also followed the *MTL* official page and your EIC."

A part of me was flattered, but an even bigger part of me was horrified that he'd somehow discovered that I had him blocked and was grasping at relevant straws to stay connected to me in some kind of way. And of course, I'd been mugging, playing happy, on the *MTL* IG stories whenever our intern turned the camera my way because I didn't need the world—or at least our following, speculating on what was going on in my life that could have me down and out. If he saw any of that he probably thought I was the most heartless bitch in these streets, unaffected by what had happened between us.

"Don't tell me that, Tee. Now I feel even worse," I groaned.

"You shouldn't," Tina said, "Don't ever feel bad for taking the time to check in with yourself when it comes to any interpersonal relationships. I know you're the self-love guru or whatever, but I've been around the block enough times and have borne witness to you transforming enough lives to know that much. If you had turned a blind eye to his past behavior and dove headfirst into something with him, I definitely would have been looking at you sideways."

"So...I shouldn't try to get that old thang back is what you're saying?" I asked, confused.

"No, girl. That is not what I'm saying at all. I'm just saying...girl I don't know shit you done confused me. Don't you always say not to take advice from your single friends?"

"I *am* the single friend who stays giving advice, so you know I ain't said that!"

"The both of y'all are nuts," Corin laughed.

"Oh...that must've been ol girl who proclaimed to be a relationship expert then lied to us all about still being married as she fought through an embittered divorce proceeding. My bad, cuz. I get all of you influencers mixed up."

"Shut up, Tina." I giggled at her shading a competitor of mine who stayed throwing barbs at me online.

"I have it on good authority that your man will be at

home alone this weekend, most likely drowning his sorrows in beer and still licking his wounds," Corin said, "You might wanna plead your case in person?"

"I can't just FaceTime him like old times and act like nothing has happened huh?"

"Uh no," Corin and Tina said in unison.

"You don't have to do any grand gesture or make a big ordeal of it, but I do think it would work better...coming from you in person. I mean, you dismissed him face to face, might as well let him know y'all can get that old thang back the same way, you know?"

"Wait, driving out to Lakeland isn't a grand gesture? Y'all know how I *hate* driving."

"You could Amtrak it up, but then if you do that and show up to his doorstep in an Uber from their train station, might be a lil awkward if he happens to not be home once you arrive. Because then what do you do? Take an Uber back to the train station or sit on his doorstep like an orphan 'til he arrives again? If he even comes straight back because what if he decided to take an impromptu trip down here to visit with CoCo and Wes?" Tina spouted off these scenarios not really convincing me to actually want to make the trip up to Lakeland.

Rux would be back down here in a few weeks for Pen's birthday party extravaganza, maybe I should just bide my time and wait until then. We'd already been apart a few weeks, what was two or three more?

As if she could see the wheels turning in my head, Corin shook her head, "Nope. Cancel whatever you're thinking because I'm tired of seeing the both of y'all walk around miserable. The drive goes by a lot faster than you'd think despite it being a near three-hour haul. Get over yourself, make some fire playlists, get thine hind parts up to Lakeland and get your man back."

With those parting words, the two of them gathered their things and left me alone with my thoughts. Co was right about me needing to speak to Rux in person. Our last conversation left me with a knotted stomach, twisted brain and mounds of confusion, but I'd hoped...this conversation would be a bit easier to have as I'd be letting go of a lot of preconceived notions and allowing us to begin fresh—with a clean slate. I grabbed my phone, navigating to first Twitter and Facebook to unblock him then ending with Instagram. Unblocking him on Instagram I saw that he'd actually been pretty active posting in the past few weeks, mostly sharing snaps of his in-progress projects or adorable pictures and videos of Harlow. If I didn't know any better, I'd think he had been getting along fine, as none of that misery that Tina and Corin had alluded to was present on his public timeline at all. He hadn't updated stories in the past twenty-four hours, so I couldn't even creep on him properly. I'd be seeing him soon enough, however, since I decided to make my way to Lakeland tomorrow afternoon.

[***]

"Are you sure he's going to be here?" I asked Corin for what had to be the fiftieth time in the past twenty minutes.

"Do you want me to hang up on your ass?"

"Testy, testy..."

"Yes or no?"

"Co!"

"You're on the next to last of my unfrayed nerves. For the very last time, yes Teddy is at home. Yes, he is there alone. No, he does not have Harlow for a couple days. And by my estimations you should have arrived a smooth fifteen minutes ago, so where pray tell are you, love?"

"Sittingoutsidehishouse," I mumbled under my breath.

"I'm sorry you're where?" Corin asked.

By her tone I should have known not to repeat myself, however I wasn't in the right frame of mind, so I foolishly repeated myself and was met with silence before the tone that indicated that our call had been disconnected sounded throughout my speaker system. With my last means of procrastination completely burnt – Tina had been put me on the block list – I got out of my car slowly, like I was making the same walk that John Coffey made. I couldn't quite place my uneasiness, since by all estimations when I rang his door-bell, Rux should be happy to see me, but that didn't stop the butterflies from doing the tootsie roll in my belly.

When I reached his front door, I inhaled a large breath, slowly exhaling as I pressed his doorbell. A few moments passed before I could hear movement behind the door, unlocking the deadbolt and opening the front and storm doors. Rux's large frame took up damn near the entire door-frame as he stood, unmoving for half a second before snatching me up and taking my mouth in a kiss that rivaled the one that he'd laid on me that first time we met in person at Corin and Wes'. I was powerless to do much more than melt into him, trying to match the fervor of his mouth against mine. When breathing became a necessity he pulled back, disconnecting our mouths as he still held me aloft, flush with his body.

I blinked stupidly, before biting down on my lip and whispering, "Hey."

One of Rux's brows quirked in response before his low voice rumbled, "Whassup Kailene."

"Can I come in or…?"

"Yeah…yeah," Rux said hurriedly, letting me down to walk through the door on my own two feet, but still crowding me pretty closely.

I'd obviously never been in his place but used intuition to

lead me from the foyer to the living room and sat down on the couch. Rux stood in the doorframe staring at me with a wide-eyed, awe-stricken look on his face as if I were an aberration or figment of his imagination. I had to laugh at the optics of this situation. I didn't know what I expected, but him stupefied into being mute wasn't quite it.

"So...what's new?" I asked.

Those few words seemed to spur him back into action as he strolled over to the couch, sat down, and ran one of those big hands of his down my face gently.

"Ok wait...you're like for real here right? Because I saw you on the app, opened the door and you were standing there, but this doesn't...still feel quite real."

Reaching up to the hand of his that was on my face, I nipped a small piece of his skin, giving him one of those good ol' mother of the church pinches that made him yelp.

"Shit!"

"You still see me?" I smirked.

"Cute...real cute, Kailene."

"You were the one who thought you were dreaming, just wanted to ensure that you weren't."

"What are you doing here? Wait...that sounds like I'm not happy to see you. Which, I'm not. I'm *extremely* happy to see you, beautiful. Especially considering..." he trailed off, looking down on me with an indecipherable look. It was a cross between wonder, confusion, and outright shock.

"We...needed to talk, so I figured we might as well do it in person."

"And you drove...*here*?"

"I did."

"By yourself."

"I'm a big girl."

"Not doubting that at all, sweetheart. I just know you *absolutely hate* driving. So...I...you wanted to talk?"

"Yeah," I said, pulling back from his hold a bit, "I do."

I sat up, crossing my legs—pulling one booted foot to rest beneath my calf as I turned further in his direction. I said nothing as I took in his appearance, a bit haggard at the moment—his beard was further overgrown than I'd ever seen it before, and his hair was a fuzzy bush of curls in need of a shape up. Rux's eyes which were normally full of guile-less optimism were guarded and wary, as if he was unsure what sent me to his doorstep.

I opened my mouth to tell him about how I'd been wrestling with my decision over the past few weeks, but instead what tumbled out was, "God, I've missed you."

Rux lowered his forehead to mine, placing a tender kiss on my nose, "I've missed you, too, sweetheart. More than you could ever know. If you've come here to tell me that this is the end for real, can you just do it quickly? Rip it off like a Band-Aid."

"Rux, I—God no. I'd come here to tell you that I'm done being miserable without you. And I...we can't forget any of what led us to this moment right now, but what we can do is proceed forward—eyes open and work toward...*building*."

I'd barely aspirated the last syllable before Rux wrapped me up in another one of those breath-robbing kisses, rendering me powerless to do much more than acquiesce to his will, melting into his embrace as he controlled my mouth with powerful strokes of his tongue lapping in my mouth. He was using this kiss, I imagined, to say all of the things left unsaid between the two of us while we were apart, and I *gladly* welcomed his impassioned plea.

When we finally pulled apart, I couldn't help but crack, "So...I'm guessing that you're willing to give this another go?"

"Understatement of the year, sweetheart."

TWELVE

RUX

I f anyone would have told me that when I woke up yesterday morning that I'd end the day with the woman I'd been making myself sick over missing comfortably enveloped in my arms...*in my bed*, I would have called them fifty flavors of liar. But as I laid here watching the even rising and falling of her chest, hearing the slight snore she emitted on every third exhalation – I felt luckier than I deserved. I let her go and *she came back*. I was convinced that we were going to be relegated to existing in a cloud of forced, awkward interactions at Wes and Rinny's and had been trying to reconcile this fact, but...now Kailene was *mine again*. I was going to have to make sure to find a church home to drop an extra-large donation in their collection plate because the man upstairs was truly looking out for me. Nothing short of divine intervention placed the benevolence on her heart needed to look past all of my fuckboy behavior and give me a chance to prove that I was worthy of her time, space, energy and eventual love.

I didn't want to get up for fear of disturbing the sleep she'd finally eased into after we'd spent most of last night up talking about everything we'd seen, done, and thought in the weeks apart. It was honestly like a pause button had been pressed during the time that we'd been apart, as we picked right back up where we left off...falling back into the same easy energy that had made the natural progression of our connection move so seamlessly the first time. This time, though, as she had requested last night, we were moving forward with our eyes wide open—being completely upfront and honest with one another, ensuring that the lines of communication remained open.

"You know it's wild creepy to just stare at someone while they're sleeping right?" Kailene suddenly spoke up, drawing my attention back toward actually focusing on her face.

I'd zoned out a bit, completely unaware that she'd awakened and was now turned on her side, facing me, cradling her chin in her hand as she smirked.

"Man, I was just tryna figure out how such a powerful sound came from such a slight body. You know you snore like a grown man with a third shift job at the local refinery, love?"

"Oh my God, I do not, shut up!" Kailene giggled, slapping me across the chest.

"I was just sitting here trying to figure out how we can make this work going forward, might have to retreat to separate rooms after we're done taking care of business, mama."

"Whatever," she drawled, rolling over and attempting to leave the bed.

Before she could complete the maneuver, I dropped a hand to her hip, "Where you going?"

"To see a man about a horse."

"Without giving me a proper good morning greeting?"

Her eyebrow quirked.

"Gimme two secs," she said scurrying from the bed before I could catch her again.

By the time I reacted and followed her out of my bedroom, she'd made her way to the living room to grab her bag we brought in late last night, retrieved her toothbrush and was in the half bath in the front of my house brushing feverishly. I chuckled, rubbing a hand over my beard as I rested against the doorframe waiting for her to finish up. After rinsing her mouth with the tiny bottle of mouthwash she'd taken out of her toiletry bag, she turned around, crooking a finger at me to come closer. I walked right up on her, lowering my head slowly until our mouths were mere inches apart.

"Good morning," she murmured before inching up on her tip toes to bring our mouths together, taking the lead on the kiss as she laced her fingers together behind my neck.

She softly pressed her lips against mine once, twice before gently sliding her tongue along the seam where my lips met, seeking entrance I damn sure wasn't denying her. Once our tongues touched, I gave up the ghost of trying to let her maintain control of this kiss. Securing my hands under her ass I hoisted Kailene into the air, positioning her exactly where I needed her to be without needing to be hunched over to meet her at the just slightly over six inches in height she lacked when we stood toe to toe. After a few moments I pulled back from the kiss, still cradling Kailene in my hands as she blushed, trying to bury her face into my neck.

"Don't get all shy on me now, mama."

"How are you just...effortlessly holding me up?"

"Girl you weigh a smooth buck fifty. *Light work*. I lift more weight than you on a low effort gym day. Question though..."

"Hmmm?"

"How long did you plan on hanging out with me?" I asked, walking us out of the small bathroom, back toward my bedroom where I deposited Kailene on the bed and crashed onto the mattress alongside her.

"Just a couple days. I actually have to get back to Belleview before Thursday because my team and I are head out to Cali for *MTL Weekend*."

"Cool, cool. Low's been missing your presence and since I'm supposed to pick her up tonight, so I figured…" I trailed off at the pained look at appeared on Kailene's face, "Uh… why the face?"

"Huh?" she deflected.

"When I mentioned Harlow…you looked like you'd just swallowed some bad sushi. Is…there something we need to talk about here?"

"No…nah, we're good," she forced a smile, "What were you saying?"

I shook my head, "Nah, mama. Remember that part about us saying whatever we needed to say whether or not we thought the other person wanted to hear it?"

"I do."

"So?"

Kailene sat up, running a hand through her hair and gnawing at her bottom lip before she opened her mouth to formulate a response. She started to speak but thought better of it before biting down on her lip and clearing her throat before beginning to speak again. I said nothing, giving her the space to figure out what the hell she wanted to say and how she wanted to phrase it. I was sure it had nothing to do with baby girl since they'd already made each other's acquaintance and were already on good terms.

"Ok, I just want you to let me say everything I need to say before you respond. And actually, *listen* to what I'm saying and not what you may hear when I say this okay?"

I nodded for her to continue.

"Maybe...we should cool it on having me hang out with you and Harlow for any extended periods of time."

"So...you want me to limit the amount of time I spend with, my baby girl?"

"That's not what I said, *Theodore*. And I asked that you hear me out before you started jumping to conclusions. Now, as I was saying before I was so rudely interrupted," she faked an annoyed pout, "after everything you told me about you and Harlow's mama...I just think we should have slow rolled this a bit. Like...circumstances what they were and yes, you introduced me to Harlow as your friend, but...the kid isn't stupid, Rux. If I'm a permanent fixture around here whenever she is here, it'll eventually trickle back to her mother, who you already said wasn't really feeling her being around me without us not having met before and..."

"Okay, so you can roll with me when I pick LowLow up from Britt's and I can introduce..."

Kailene held up a hand, halting my speech, "Still wasn't finished. I know your aunt and uncle taught you better manners than that, man. Sheesh. Anyway...this has nothing to do with Harlow...*or her mama*...and everything to do with me. Like...okay...again don't take offense, but this doesn't seem kinda add water and mix, instant family to you? Britt didn't work, but you've found a lady that you're clicking with, so you can just plug and play me into y'alls lives."

My head reared back at that comment and the implications it held, "Ain't nobody trying to make you an instant mom, Kailene."

"Okay," she said, holding her hands up in acquiescence, "that's fine. I believe you. But...we won't be introducing me to Britt, and I will be on my way back to Belleview before you leave to pick up Harlow tomorrow though."

"Do you...not want to be around my daughter?"

"Did I say that?"

"This little speech and your actions right now are pretty much saying that for you, so," I shrugged, "I don't really see how you think this would be sustainable as Harlow spends several nights a week over here and every other weekend. If we're doing the long-distance thing, that already severely limits our time and if you're expecting to only be around when Low isn't here..."

"I feel like I'm not being clear. Or maybe you're being purposefully obtuse and are tryna bait me into a disagreement. I don't know. What I do know is that this?" she gestured with her hands back and forth between the two of us, "it's not working for me. So, if there's something you don't get about what I'm saying, you can ask me to clarify myself instead of withdrawing and pouting your way through what I thought was a civilized discussion we were about to have."

"Time out, nobody's pouting, man. And as far as you being unclear, I'm sayin', any objection you had to my daughter could have been raised in the weeks during which *you* began bonding with *her* as *we* bonded," I said, rolling from on my side facing Kailene to lying flat on my back staring up at the ceiling.

"There's my entire point right there, baby," Kailene said softly, resting her chin on my chest, "I shouldn't have even been allowed to bond with her that early. Okay, wait...let's take a step back. Let's say Britton had been talking to a man for a few weeks and had him around Harlow without reservation in that short time period. You know nothing about the dude, but he and your baby got inside jokes and been yukking it up from the beginning. You wouldn't feel a way about that?"

"So...this *is* about Britt?"

"No! And I asked you a question."

"I'd trust Britt's judgement that she wouldn't have my

147

baby around no sucka ass dude. Plus, this isn't the same. You're not a stranger danger ass dude coming into the picture. We damn near family."

Kailene grimaced at that.

"Not family, but...you know...it ain't the same, Kailene."

"To you!" she exclaimed, "but it's the exact same concept to Britt, babe. And she had to hear about daddy's new girlfriend via her child which makes it worse. I'm not saying that I don't want to be around Harlow. I'd never say that because you all are raising a delightful little drop of brown sugar. What I am saying, however, is that what if we never recovered from our little break? It's not just us affected here. She is affected, too...and that doesn't sit right with me. But I can't help but think...if we'd slow rolled this, brought Harlow into the equation *after* we'd established something solid then..."

And there it was. Now it was clicking for me. This wasn't about me, Britt, or Kailene. This was about the one person beyond Kailene who should have been handled more carefully in this situation that I'd completely put into a place to be hurt and I didn't think twice about it. I was smitten, caught up in this exploration of something new with Kailene that it didn't even occur to me that there would be a chance of us suffering such a breakdown that it would adversely affect my baby girl. She'd asked after Kailene in the weeks since we'd been apart, and I always came up with an excuse about work keeping her busy in order to keep from having to share with my daughter how we'd – Kailene and I – made a mess of things. That was information to which she needn't be privy, but also would not have been necessary for me to keep from her had I perhaps slowed my brakes when it came to bringing all parts of my world together so quickly.

"Message received. And I'm sorry, for blowing this out of proportion. I understand exactly where you'd coming from now...and that's my bad. I guess the...excitement of us coming together seeming like some ordained by the cosmos type shit had me getting a little… carried away. My bad."

"Was that our first official fight as a couple?" Kailene chuckled, biting down on that damn lower lip again.

I guided a hand to rest below her chin, angling her face toward mine, "Yeah, I guess so. You forgive me?"

She shook her head, "Nah…I like my apologies in the form of breakfast foods. And since I never got any of these world-famous waffles I had to keep hearing about from CoCo and Pen…"

I chuckled, "Say less, sweetheart."

I urged her to follow me out of bed and toward the kitchen as I made sure I had everything I needed to introduce her to my one and only culinary claim to fame. Cooking was something that I'd been forced to step my game up with once Harlow became a regular fixture at my place. Britt wasn't with the constant fast food consumption and baby girl's palate wasn't exactly refined enough to appreciate fine dining experiences, so I turned to the internet to help me learn how to cook some simple, quick meals for the days when I would be responsible for feeding Harlow more than a quick snack. While I prepped our breakfast, Kailene showered and got dressed since she declared that after breakfast, I needed to show her all of the hot spots in Lakeland. I'd never heard a more oxymoronic statement, but I promised to do my best. Moving here, further out in the sticks than I was used to living in had been a change in scenery for me for sure.

Growing up in Belleville wasn't exactly the big city, but it was a suburb just outside of the city, so I'd had plenty of access to city living before I moved to Lakeland to attend undergrad and promptly received a job that I was sure would eventually have me on a fast track to living in the city. I never quite used that job in the steppingstone manner as I got comfortable being a big dog in a small yard, ascending through the ranks of being a lowly associate to junior partner quickly. I made decent money, had a low overhead and didn't want to give that up to be making the same amount of money while paying a premium for being in the thick of it all. My life here afforded me the ability to be able to make moves that would prove long term beneficial.

It also afforded me the ability to not be under the watchful eye of my Aunt Lane as I maneuvered through dating, post undergrad. Since Wes and Rinny had damn near been predetermined from the beginning of time, she never gave him much grief about women, but me? Man, she stayed on my head. *When are you gonna settle down? When you gonna give me some grandbabies, too?* Swear Harlow had been a saving grace in more ways than one when I ran into her and Britt. Auntie was immediately smitten with my mini me and got off my back about ceasing to sow my wild oats and laying down roots. Crazy how that was something I'd thought was years off, but in a matter of weeks I was starting to regret where I'd begun building that foundation. I didn't want to put the cart before the horse or however that saying went but...Kailene was...definitely somebody I could see myself with for the long haul. Yet another thing that would have surprised anybody in my life had I said it a mere six months ago. But it was my truth.

Kailene and I fell back into our routine of nonstop caking, as Wes liked to call it, almost immediately once we'd reconciled. I had to be cognizant of her wishes to stay low when it came to interacting with Harlow as we worked toward actually claiming each other in public or whatever, but in these past couple of months we'd managed to grow closer. I ended up in Belleville for Penelope's birthday and we got to spend a good chunk of quality time together, holed up in our own little world until duty called and I needed to get back to Lakeland. It felt...almost blasphemous to say something like this because admitting this to anyone beyond myself...and my therapist would seem fucked up beyond belief, but in addition to be incredibly attracted to Kailene I *liked her* as a person. That wasn't to say that I did not like any woman with whom I'd bonded prior to this connection, but Kailene was the first time that I actually allowed myself to let a woman in completely. Dr. Philips gave me some line about how that was emblematic of growth, but I honestly attributed it to Kailene more than myself. She was effortlessly magnetic, the type of woman that everyone wanted to be or befriend—intelligent but not pompous about it, strikingly gorgeous but self-effacing, much preferring to let someone else have the spotlight despite being wholly deserving of it. She had a corny sense of humor and my dad jokes had a breadth a mile long with her, always bringing forth that pretty ass smile or a peal of laughter. She was just...*it*, the whole package—full stop.

And she finally felt comfortable enough to meet Britton, so I was currently waiting for her to pull into town and then in a few hours—me, Kailene, Harlow, Britton, and her dude had dinner plans. Some shit that I wasn't really into, but it was something that Kailene insisted upon. Surprisingly Britt readily agreed, insisting on hosting us at her place instead of all of us going out for dinner. I definitely wasn't trying to have that shit, but Kailene told me that I was being paranoid. *Let her extend this olive branch*, she urged when I told her about these amended plans. *It'll be fine.* Felt like some bullshit to me, but Kailene was convinced that there was no malicious intent underlying. As for me? I'd be keeping my eyes and ears peeled. Britt was good at acting one way in one instance then flipping the script in the blink of an eye. I didn't want to be walking myself and Kailene into an eventual ambush situation. My phone sounded off and I picked it up to see the object of my current thoughts had just sent a text.

Open the door! — Kbae ♥

I wasn't expecting her to be here this early, so I opened the door with a confused expression etched across my features.

"What're you doing here?" I said, grabbing her bags with one hand and pulling her into my body with the other as she entered my house.

"Am…I not supposed to be here?" she sassed, pecking my lips quickly.

Dropping her bag just inside the foyer, I led us to the couch, "Now ain't nobody said all that. Hell, I'm just waiting for you to stop frontin' and…"

"And…?" Kailene prodded.

"Nah, I can't be giving up all my secrets yet. But for real, I thought you wouldn't be here 'til closer to the time that we needed to be on our way to Britt's, not that I'm complaining."

"Baby, what time do you think it is?"

At that I glanced down at my watch to see that it was at least three hours later than I thought it was. I'd been so caught up in getting some work handled that I'd clearly lost track of time.

"Shit, I still need to shower," I said, running a hand over my face, "You uh…ready for this?"

"Me? Are *you* ready for this?" Kailene giggled, "This yo' baby mama drama."

"Aw here you go…"

I got up to get my ass in the shower, brushing off Kailene's offer to wash my back with a promise to let her do more than that once we were done with dinner. I knew damn well that if I let her anywhere near me beforehand? We wouldn't be making it anywhere. I made quick work of showering and dressing, so we could roll over to Britt's.

While I was getting dressed, Kailene filled me in on the latest drama between two managing editors at *More to Life* and all of the petty arguments between them that she's had to referee since she'd been in the office more.

She tried to act like she was annoyed, but I could tell that she enjoyed how much her staff really relied on her presence as more than a figurehead. I loved hearing her talk about her work because I could tell that she was truly enamored with what she had created. And she should be based on the hordes of folks who sung her praises on the internet. After I got my self together, we rolled out to Britt's, but Kailene seemed a little reticent on the drive over. I said nothing, knowing she'd eventually say whatever was on her mind after she'd mulled it over to the point of no longer being able to contain herself. So, I simply reached over with the hand that wasn't steering and laced her fingers with mine, bringing our joined hands up to my mouth to plant a soft kiss on top of hers. We'd been driving for about three minutes in silence before Kailene spoke up again.

"No for real though, you're good, right? I know this has been something you've been pushing for a minute..."

"I'm glad you're *finally* comfortable with this happening."

"Yeah," she said distractedly, looking out of the window.

"Hey," I said, squeezing her hand to draw her attention back to me, "you...*are* comfortable with this right? Like you don't feel like I've been pushing the issue too hard?"

I'd been cognizant of her feelings about me trying to rush her into things when she wasn't quite ready. It was a thing that she brought up intermittently and I had to check my enthusiasm before it ended up pushing her further away. Kailene, for all of her sagacity and wisdom doled out to other was a very slow and methodical person when it came to making moves in her own life. It was amazing to witness, honestly, how she could be so decisive in her professional life, but when it came to her personal life she moved with such…caution. We'd not yet really dove too deep into the source of why she moved this way, but I could definitely just about guess that it had something to do with some dude in her past.

"No," she quickly reassured, "I don't think you're pushing anything. You actually fell all the way back with that and I appreciate you giving me my space to work things through on my own. I know you probably think I'm putting on the brakes on a lot, but I promise I just like to be…sure…*certain* before taking and making certain leaps. I am, however, full disclosure, a little nervous with what to expect with Britton though since you said she can be on her Jekyll and Hyde from time to time."

"You know if she jumps out the box, I'm stepping up for you, baby. No question."

"Never a doubt in my mind," Kailene grinned, "I just… don't want it to be ugly or awkward in front of Low."

"Well from what I can see Britt and her dude are on solid ground so she shouldn't have too much smoke for me or you right now."

"What is this guy's name? You stay referring to him as dude or buddy."

"Honestly, baby, because I cannot remember if dude's name is Glenn or Greg. I just know it begins with a G," I laughed, "And I didn't wanna ask LowLow to tell me his name for the fourth time."

"Oh my god, Rux, *no*…"

"So hopefully she introduces buddy by name to you when we pull up…otherwise I'ma just keep on calling him my man whenever we interact."

"Has that been…often? You guys interacting I mean?"

"Not really. Sometimes he's there when I pick up Low from Britt's or drop her back off, but he stays in the background, plays his part. Hell, lowkey this is a little test for me too, to see where buddy's head is at with my shorty around, you know? Not that I think Britt has bad judgement, but…"

"Is this the same guy from when…you know?"

I shook my head, "Nah, this is actually her high school sweetheart, believe it or not. They randomly reconnected and been giving it another go. That's about as much as she was willing to share with me though…understandably."

Soon, we were pulling in front of Britt's house and our conversation wound down. Getting out of the car, I grabbed the cake that Kailene had insisted upon bringing, some sort of sweet potato bourbon bundt situation that smelled good as hell when she'd moved it from her car to mine. That was something I hadn't known about her, this baking talent, which she informed me was something she did to clear her mind or ease her nerves. Even while we walked up to the house, I could still feel some tension radiating from her despite her saying she was cool. We were barely three steps onto the walkway that led up to Britt's door when it flew open and Harlow came running out.

"Miss Kai, you caaaaame!" Harlow exclaimed, completely ignoring me and damn near taking Kailene out at the knees as she ran to give her a huge hug.

"Hey, lil mama! Of course, I did, how can I resist an invite to hang out with my favorite nail buddy? In fact…speaking of nails, I got something for you when we get inside."

Harlow hit a quick lil dance move excited about whatever Kai had for her, something of which I wasn't even aware as I muttered, "you didn't have to bring her anything, babe."

Kailene spoke through her teeth, still smiling, "I'm aware."

"Harlow Marie, what have I told you about opening my door when no one is around?" Britton snapped from the doorway.

"But mama, I saw my daddy and Miss Kai coming up and I just wanted to…"

"What did I tell you?" Brit gritted out.

Harlow turned her eyes my way beseechingly, but all I could do was shrug.

"You know your mama's rules, peanut."

Harlow walked back in the direction of the house where her mama was still fussing with Kailene and I trailing her. I tried not to laugh at the way she dragged, like she was on her way to a sentencing when all it was actually going to be was Britt harping on her for a few minutes before she let up. Harlow, however, didn't like to get those stern types of talking to in front of company, deeply embarrassed by being chastised.

I tuned back in to hear Britt saying, "Now get your little narrow tail back in there and finish helping Gil set the table."

"His name is Gil. You were nowhere near close," Kailene whispered, barely containing her giggle.

I shrugged again, shooting Kailene a quick grin before nodding in Britton's direction, "Hey BM, this is my girl Kailene. Kailene, this is Harlow's mama, Britton."

Kailene stuck out a hand for a shake, "Nice to meet you, Britton."

Britt held up her hands which were covered in flour, "I would shake but I'm running a little behind on dinner and am still tryna finish up these biscuits, but it's nice to meet you too. Come on in, y'all, I'll have Gil fix some drinks while I'm finishing up in the kitchen."

She didn't give either us a chance to reply before she turned on a heel and dashed back into the kitchen. Moments later her significant other appeared, carrying a couple glasses a bottle of wine and a corkscrew.

"What up, man?" the guy I now knew to be named Gil

said, coming over to dap me up once he set the things in his hands down on the table.

"Everything is everything, Gil. How about you?"

"Man, I can't call it. I'm glad we're finally getting a chance to do this though. I told Britt we shoulda been had you out to the crib to break bread."

"Everything in its due time, right? My bad, I ain't even introduced my lady. Gil, this is my girl Kailene. Baby, this is Britt's guy, Gil."

They shook hands and we all stood there for an awkward moment before sitting down on the couches in the sitting room. Gil turned on the television and we pretended to be paying attention to the rerun of Criminal Minds that was playing before he made an excuse to go back into the kitchen with Britt.

"My man, before you take off, Kailene brought dessert you mind taking this with you?"

Gil nodded his assent, grabbing the cake dish from me as he walked out of the room.

"This should be interesting, huh?" I said with a raise of my brows toward Kailene and she just smirked.

Before she could reply, Harlow burst back into the room asking if she could have her surprise now. Kai dug into the large bag that was perched upon her shoulder, pulling out a small giftbag with a glittery unicorn emblazoned on the side of it. Harlow was so enamored with the bag, gushing over the sparkly unicorn horn for a good ninety seconds before ripping the tissue paper out of the bag and uncovering her treasure.

"Nail polish! Ohmigod, thank you Miss Kai!" she shrieked, before running back into the kitchen to show her mother, "Mama look what Miss Kai brought me!"

"It's specially made for kids, nontoxic and just in case she finds herself nibbling at her nails, totally edible," Kailene said to me, "I…hope that's okay?"

"You know it's fine with me, baby. Now her mama on the other hand?" I chuckled.

Britton had damn near flipped her wig when I brought Harlow back from Belleview with a little manicure after Aunt Lane's party, reading me the damned riot act. I think it was because she assumed, wrongly, that this was something that she and Kailene had done together. Once Harlow actually let her mama know that she'd gotten her nails does with her cousin Penny, Britt was miraculously less upset about her baby having her nails done.

"You think I overstepped? I figured this would be a good compromise for the both of them. She…or you can paint Low's nails on command and not have to come out of any money at a real shop. I…shit," Kailene swore lowly, inhaling sharply.

"Babe, relax. I was just messing with you. I think Britt had bought her some little kiddie makeup kit that had some little polishes in it already, so you're adding to an already existing collection. You're fine."

Kailene swatted me across the chest, "You play too much! You really had me thinking she was finna come out of that kitchen and read me the riot act for overstepping my bounds with her baby."

"Aight, y'all, I think we're finally ready to eat," Britt called out and we walked into her dining area.

Looking at the place settings I had to chuckle to myself a little bit. Britt had a small six-seater, with settings for her and Gil at either end, but instead of placing mine and Kailene's settings alongside one another there was one place set for an adult and then one for a kid on one side of the table and one lonely spot set on the other. I saw Kailene's facial expression narrow at the table briefly before she shook her head. I didn't say shit, but ushered Kai to the seat next to Harlow and took the one on the opposite side. Where I'd chosen to sit placed Kailene between Low and Gil, which I was sure wasn't Britt's intention at all given the surprised look on her face when she came out to join us at the table. I prayed she wasn't on any bullshit tonight, but in all honesty, I couldn't be too sure with Britton. My fears, however, were completely unfounded as we made it through dinner and dessert unscathed. We ended up hanging out for a while at Britt's though we'd only initially committed to staying until Harlow went down, but once Gil brought out the cards and brown liquor the night ended up in us sitting around shooting the breeze and talking shit over a game of Spades long after Low had nodded off at the table and Britt went and put her to bed.

Once Britt put together that Kailene was the founder of *More to Life* the conversation took a turn, as she gushed over how much she loved the website and how it was partially responsible for bringing her and Gil back together. She told us the story about how she'd read an article on the site about making amends with past lovers in order to fully move forward without reservation when seeking out future relationships. Shortly before Britton had read that article, she and Gil had randomly reconnected via social media and she saw that article as a sign that she needed to directly engage him. Unfortunately that was also around the time shit between her and me went south the second time, which brought about an awkward lull in the conversation before Britt continued the story, telling us how they were just trying to be friends, but one thing led to another and now here they were...together and...happy. Something I could honestly see on the both of their faces now that I was paying close enough attention to how they interacted—the softening of their eyes when their gazes met, the subtle ways they filled in the gaps for one another as Britt told their tale, the broad grins stretching both of their faces.

Soon, I could tell that Kailene was feeling the effects of her earlier drive, with the subtle yawns she tried hiding behind her hand as the night wore on. Britt finally let us go, with the urgent insistence that we made this something that we'd do regularly. We made loose plans and headed out the door, but Britt grabbed me by the arm before I could fully cross the threshold.

"Can I...borrow him for a minute, Kai?" she asked, sorta meekly which was the complete opposite of her normal demeanor.

"Sure," Kailene smiled, "It's unlocked, right babe?"

I nodded before pressing the key fob once more just to be double sure. Once Kailene walked off I turned to Britt expectantly.

"I like her a lot. And *I like her for you.* Don't fuck this up, Theodore."

"Okay who are you and what the hell have you done with my baby mama?" I joked.

"I'm *serious*," Britt doubled down, "Look I know things between us were whatever they were but one thing reconnecting with Gil has taught me is the power of forgiveness. We—you and me—were *never* supposed to be. Not like this anyway. You and her, however? Like I said, don't fuck it up, man."

"Aight, BM."

"Hey! I told you to stop calling me that."

"What? You don't like being called by your initials, Britton Martin?" I teased.

"They won't be my initials much longer, actually," she said, reaching into her shirt and pulling out the chain she'd been wearing around her neck to hold it up and show me a ring, "Never quite found a way to work this into our convo tonight, but…"

I whistled at the sizeable rock that caught a bit of the porch light and glittered as Britt held it aloft. I was definitely shocked, but quickly schooled my features to not show it.

"Hey, my man G ain't waste no time locking you down, huh?"

"Yeah…we've…I…I wanted to tell you first, we haven't even said anything to Harlow yet."

"Congrats, B. I mean it. Gil's a good dude. *I like him for you*," I said, mimicking her statement about Kailene.

"We've still got a little way before any ceremonies or anything will be happening, but…well…"

"This little dinner was as much for my benefit as it was yours. Mmmmhmm, I see you."

"And we're done here. Safe travels!" Britt laughed, pushing me from her front porch.

"Give Gil my condolences, I meant…congratulations," I joked walking to my car.

By the time I'd gotten in and started the car up, Kailene was completely zonked out in the passenger seat, mouth open, snoring lightly. *Guess I'd have to share Britt and Gil's good news with her in the morning*, I thought as I pulled away from the curb and navigated us home.

THIRTEEN

KAI

"**Y**ou look happy," Rux mused as we sat next to one another on my couch listlessly watching television.

"That's because *I am happy*. Supremely so. Actually, happy would be a misnomer. I am satisfied. Gratified," I purred in response, moving from being nestled into Rux's side to straddling his lap, "I am so glad you came, baby. I missed you."

He'd popped up unexpectedly, but right on time because I'd been missing him something heavy. Despite both of us having pretty...portable careers that allowed us to have flexibility to work nearly anywhere, we'd both been entirely too busy to actually coordinate any face to face time in weeks, which had me vexed. I found myself vacillating between feeling like I was doing too much too soon, but also wondering how much longer I could deal with this physical distance between us as we grew closer. We were only a few months into being *official*, but the one thing that I knew for certain was that this thing with Rux, however unconventional and unexpected, was one of the best things to happen to me in recent history. I still couldn't believe that not only had I placed a personal ad in the paper, but the fact that the man I had been looking for this whole time was in arm's reach. The universe had hella jokes.

Cradling my face between his two oversized palms, Rux brought our faces together speaking right against my lips when he growled, "I've been missing you too, sweetheart. You have no idea how badly."

"Oh, I can feel...how much you've missed me," I giggled, rolling my hips against his growing erection, "Come on, let me show you and my friend just how much y'all have been missed."

"Why we gotta go anywhere?" Rux crooned, nipping at my neck to punctuate his words.

I said nothing in return, just inclined my head to give him better access as he trailed his mouth along the side of my neck, his hands moving from my waist to gather the hem of my shirt and pull it over my head. The surprised, yet thankful groan he let out when he realized I wasn't wearing a bra so he had direct access to my breasts made me giggle, a sound that didn't last long before it morphed into a moan as he took one stiffened nipple, then the other into his mouth.

"All on the couch? Really, Kailene!" Tina chastised and I leapt from Rux's lap, haphazardly draping my shirt across my naked upper half.

Rux's chuckle as Tina kept tutting as if she wasn't the interloper here just made me even more keyed up.

"Why are you here, Celestine?" I grumbled.

"Um, you were the one insistent on me coming to keep you company since your man had abandoned you and CoCo and her family were out of town? Did I hallucinate that pitiful ass phone call with you wailing this morning? Was it a fever dream?"

"You make me sick," I whined, burying my hands in my face, "And you talk too much."

"As you can see though…occupied now," I gestured to Rux who was just staring at the two of us with an amused smirk on his face.

"Hey, Rux," Tina grinned, "I should go?"

"Whassup, Tee?" Rux laughed, "My bad, I ain't mean to interrupt any plans y'all had. I didn't tell Kailene I was comin in this week…"

"See, sister-cousin, I told you he wasn't just tired of your ass," Tina teased.

"Please stop telling all of my business. Actually…you can just…" I motioned toward the door in a shooing motion.

"Okay, I can take a hint, I know when I'm not wanted, but…I did forget to bring your Pigalles back for the joint next week. Sorry, sis – I think I left them on that little table in my foyer. Call me later?"

I nodded and then as quickly as she appeared Tina was gone and I groaned loudly.

"I'm never gonna hear the end of this. And I know she's gonna tell my mama and Auntie Didi that she walked in on me riding you reverse cowgirl because there's nothing Tee loves more than embellishing and embarrassing me. This… this right here was why I suggested we move this party else-where. My people stay popping up at my house unan-nounced and unprovoked."

"She said you asked her to come over though?" Rux asked.

"I…don't recall any of the sort," I deflected, not wanting to address the truth that Tina had revealed.

I had called her this morning, freaking out because it felt like a chasm had been erected between Rux and I over the past couple of weeks because he was working on a massive project for his former employer's corporate gifting suite and I'd been traveling for *MTL* stuff, we'd been like two ships passing. We tried to not let more than a week and a half pass without us seeing each other in person, but we'd been coming up on over twenty days since we'd been close enough to touch before he rode down on me today. Tina talked me off the ledge and we tentatively planned a girls' day in to commence after she was done with her errands for the day. I'd been so excited to see Rux at my door a couple hours after she and I made those plans that I never did follow up and cancel since I was otherwise occupied.

"So...you weren't feeling neglected by me?"

"Neglected?" my voice cracked, "Who said anything about neglect? That's a crime I could never accuse you of."

"Damn right."

Rux worked hard at keeping the lines of communication open between us and also ensuring that I knew that he wasn't playing around with me. We'd yet to say the words verbally—something I was sure he was holding back due to my cautiousness, but I could tell...just by the way he cared for me, and looked at me, and talked to me...we were well on our way... merrily wallowing in love.

"I was, however," I started in a small voice, "lonely as hell. I...nevermind."

"Nope," Rux said immediately, grabbing me by the chin to make my eye contact return to his, "You know we don't do never mind. Say how you feeling, Kailene. We can't fix it without knowing what we're up against right?"

"I mean, you're right. I'm just...it's hard you know? Sometimes I just wanna be able to come home and immediately crawl up under you and just feel the warmth of your skin against mine, but the way our lives are set up now...that FaceTime don't quite hit the same."

"You know where I'm at with it, mama. All you gotta do is say yes."

"Okay, Floetry," I giggled.

"I'm serious, Kailene. My offer still stands, you know…"

"I know…I just…"

"Are a little scaredycat, I know."

I rolled my eyes, "Between you and Debra I'm about to have a complex."

"Don't be fronting on your moms," Rux cracked, "You know she's right, but I'm here to tell you that you have absolutely nothing to be scared about sweetheart. Take full confidence in the fact that I'm moving at your speed."

The last time I'd complained about our distance, Rux suggested that I move into his old condo that he still owned in Lakeland. His tenant's lease was up and wasn't being renewed, so the place was sitting vacant waiting for someone to move in. Since it was there and I thought it was way too early for me to be trying to shack up with a man, Rux offered it as a solution to have me in Lakeland and for me to still be able to maintain my own space. It was a very logical decision because with the path we were traveling down, our eventual consolidation of assets would only end up in me moving to Lakeland. Rux was the one who had more ties to the place in which he currently resided, obviously with Harlow and her mom living there. There was no way in hell I'd ever expect him to uproot his life when that relationship was so vital, and they were deeply entrenched into their routines. I was the interloper here when it came to that situation and I was wholly aware. It never even crossed my mind to ask Rux to move here, despite having built a life for myself here with the purchase of my townhome.

"I know," I breathed.

"And if you're worried about the expenses, don't. I know the landlord will cut you a deal in exchange for services…" Rux trailed off.

"Oh yeah, I'm interested in discussing the terms of these services."

Instead of replying verbally, Rux got up from the couch and threw me over his shoulder, leading us both in the direction of my bedroom, "We can discuss these terms and others...upstairs."

My reply was nothing more than a giggle, realizing that Rux not only went along with my attempt at distracting him from the heavier topic at hand here, instead acquiescing to my pivot. The offer was tempting, extremely so...but still, I hesitated. I needed to make a decision before the advertisement that he'd recently put up on the market to rent out the space was answered and my options of places to stay in Lakeland would only be one. The one that I knew for certain I wasn't quite ready to make my permanent home just yet. Though, if I really kept it real with myself, it was where I'd wanted to be if I did make the leap to move to Lakeland for an extended basis. My mind was quickly shifted to other thoughts and emotions as Rux stripped me down to nothingness and commanded my attention for the rest of the afternoon into the evening.

[***]

"You know we into it right?" Tina said as I walked into her house, my foot barely across the threshold before she started talking trash.

"What? How?"

"You and ya lil man all on social media looking like hashtag relationship goals and you got my mama in my ear talking about maybe I oughta try running a personal ad like you did in the paper so I don't die all dried up and alone."

"Noooooo," I giggled, "My te-te ain't play you out like that."

"*Did*," Tina confirmed, pulling up her phone to show me a pic of Rux and I that my aunt had forwarded her in Facebook

167

Messenger with those words as the caption. Instantly a smile spread across my face as I looked at the pic that Auntie Didi had sent Tina. It was from Pen's birthday a few weeks ago when Rux and I got a little silly with the self-timer and his graffiti wall creation when the kids were done posing for their pictures. We'd cycled through a series of poses, but the photo in question was one where Rux stood behind me, enveloping my body with his while I gazed up at him with the biggest grin on my face.

"I'm sorry, sister-cousin," I giggled, "You uh…might not wanna check your email any time soon though."

"Oh God, what now?" Tina fake grumbled, navigating to the very app I'd told her to avoid. Her face scrunched and she groaned aloud when she saw the invite that we'd sent out. "You gotta be shitting me, y'all hosting joint events now?"

I'd wanted to host my family at my place for Thanksgiving and when I brought it up to Corin she suggested that we merge our parties since Rux - and Harlow - would be down here for celebrating the holiday with their fam out at *The Estate*. It would be a good time for everyone to all come together considering that this configuration would likely be one that would be happening for the foreseeable future with the way things were progressing between Rux and I.

"Do I need to bring a date to this or will y'all just sit me at the kids table with Penny and your little stepdaughter?"

"Chill, Tee. You buggin', you know it won't even be like that."

"Oh, girl please, you know our moms are lowkey in competition with one another using our lives as fodder for one upping each other. You already had me in the professional life and now you got the black ass nerve to get your personal life together too and leave your poor cousin in the dust. Hell, I might have to take Jacques off the shelf again just so my mother doesn't start looking for nunneries to ship me off to."

"Jacques, huh?" I asked, smirking with one brow raised in askance, "That Vienna sausage must be more appetizing than you previously spoke of…"

"I mean…he has his other…*talents*, to make up for where he falls…short," Tina snickered.

"So, are you thinking of inviting him to Thanksgiving for real because if so—"

Tina cut me off, "Nope, I'm not. I was just saying. The last thing I need is for anyone in this situation to get the wrong idea about what is going on between Jacques and me. He's just…around and available to scratch any itches when I need him to be. Nothing more significant than that…and neither of us are upset about that."

"I dunno, Tee. Now that I think back on it, he did used to have a thing for you back in the day, sis. This might just be a delayed love connection."

"Chill out. It's nothing of the sort and how did we even get on this anyway?"

"You brought him up!"

"And now I'm putting him down."

There was a slight edge in her tone that let me know not to keep pushing, so I dropped it, knowing that whatever was behind this sudden…aggression would eventually come to light. Tina and I were a lot alike in that way, how we processed things occurring in our lives to the point of no return before finally opening up and letting anyone around us in to discuss the issues. I was, thankfully, getting better at not bottling things up to the point of eventual explosion thanks to this open-door communication policy that Rux and I were steadfastly adhering to. It was strange, allowing myself to be completely vulnerable with a man—and receiving that same energy in return, but I was very into it.

"What are you doing over here anyway? Ain't your man in town? Shouldn't you be somewhere up under him...literally," Tina laughed.

"He is...and I was...but now I'm over here because I came to get my Pigalles back. I'm wearing them to the event tonight that...you're still coming to, right?"

"I absolutely am coming despite, just like on Thanksgiving now too, being relegated to an additional wheel in a group full of couples."

"Oh my God, Tee. It isn't even like that. The girls will be there and our parents, totally not a couples thing."

I was being honored as an alumna of excellence at our former high school. Each year they chose notable alumni to award with these medals of honor and I was pleasantly surprised to receive a call a few weeks ago letting me know that I had been selected. The call had come from one of my favorite teachers at the time I attended who was still hanging in there, imparting knowledge to the youth. Mrs. Wallace taught all of the advanced English courses from freshman through senior level. She was a no-nonsense Black woman who commanded no less than excellence from all of the students in her classes. She was one of the first people who helped me find my voice through writing. English had never quite been one of my favorite subjects in school growing up, but I'd always had a passable command of it. I'd been more drawn to the social science electives I was allowed to take because human nature was a subject that always interested me, mightily. Who knew that I'd eventually be combining my innate talents with a passion to create an impactful sort of community?

Mrs. Wallace and I giggled quite a bit over the name of my site, which I graciously asked her to shorten to *More to Life* when it was being referenced in the written and oral summation of what I'd been doing since graduating from Taylor High School that had qualified me for this honor. I wasn't ashamed or embarrassed by what had essentially been me being flippant turning into my legacy at all, but I knew that some of the more…conservative community members would be clutching their pearls at the full name of the site.

"Man, whatever…" Tina grumbled with fake annoyance, "Like I said, we into it. Because the pressure is on tenfold from Deidre."

"Auntie is on your neck like that?"

"Enough to the point where I actually did consider bringing Jacques as a date tonight just so she would stop telling me that if I had something to tell her I could just say it. Hell, my life would probably be a lot easier if I liked the lady wimmenz sexually, I heard lesbians wife down quickly as hell."

"Celestine, please…" I groaned, giggling.

"Laugh at my pain, it's cool."

[***]

Corin had broken out the fancy china once again as we gathered – me, Rux, Harlow, my mom and dad, Auntie Didi and Uncle Duck, Tina, Corin, Wes, Pen, Mrs. Lane and Mr. Weston…and a last-minute addition of Britt and Gilbert. The earlier part of the day had been consumed with getting the meal together, with all of the women in our families piling into Corin's massive kitchen and compiling their assigned dishes. The girls cycled in and out of the kitchen all morning, little ears perking up as we allowed them privilege to sit and listen to our conversations which ran the gamut from commentary about our current political environment to random happenings in pop culture. I loved seeing the way

Pen interacted with Harlow despite their seven year age difference. Unlike most tweens she didn't mind her baby cousin following her like a shadow, they'd developed a sisterly bond, with Harlow worshiping Pen as if she held all of the secrets of the universe in her palm. They reminded me of me and Tina growing up, finding solace in each other as siblings since we were both only children.

I couldn't help but grin as I looked over at Rux as we sat at this table surrounded by our families. He and my Uncle Duck were currently engaged in a friendly back and forth about our local football team and its quarterback. Rux insisted that the kid needed a chance to prove himself while Uncle Duck said we shoulda drafted one of the many young, Black QBs who'd been available during the draft where we picked up that kid. Both of the Westons and my daddy were split between both sides, but none of them were as passionate as Uncle Duck and Rux. The ease with which Rux interacted with my family, even the incessant teasing from my uncle just endeared him more to me. I came from a family that was notoriously…with the shits…as the kids said, so having a man who could not only keep up with the verbal sparring but dish out a few barbs of his own was…refreshing.

Seeing them like this cemented the decision that I'd come to earlier in the week. I had been wrestling with it for the past couple of weeks since I'd been honored at that alumni event at my high school. That was the first time that Rux… and Harlow, had been around my family for an extended amount of time. We'd had the gala and also spent some one on one time with my parents. Rux had my mom wrapped around his finger already, but this was when he'd really won my dad over. Kenneth Alexander never believed anybody was good enough for his baby but before we'd left his house, he pulled me aside to express his approval of Rux as the man in my life.

Soon, dinner was winding down and I got up to grab one of the many desserts we'd prepared from the kitchen with a nod to Corin to follow me to the kitchen. She came in shortly after me, with Tina in tow as well.

"Is it corny that I wanna make an announcement at the table about Lakeland?" I asked, nervously nibbling on my bottom lip.

Corin yelped, "You're doing it!"

"Ayeeeee," Tina cheered, "Wait...does Rux know?"

I shook my head, "You two are the first to know that I've officially made my decision."

"Okay, wait...you gotta tell him first...before you tell anyone else," Corin insisted, grabbing Tina's arm and leading her out of the kitchen, "Like...I just feel like that moment needs to be private. Come on, Tee..."

Before I could protest the two of them left me by myself and I could hear Wes cracking about them coming back empty handed before I heard the scraping of a chair against the floor indicating someone had gotten up. Seconds later Rux walked into the kitchen, a cautiously curious expression on his face.

"What's up, babe? Rinny said you needed me asap."

"She's so damned dramatic, I swear," I giggled, "But... um...yeah I did need you. Do need you."

"Whassup, what you need?" Rux asked.

"I...um," I started, clearing the sudden frog that'd appeared in my throat, "I need you to take your condo off the rental market...if that's cool?"

I tried saying that last part breezily, but instead my voice shook like a tree rattled by a strong wind. Rux said nothing, just grinned broadly as what I'd said filtered into his consciousness.

"For real?"

I nodded, suddenly feeling too emotional to speak without my voice completely breaking.

Sweeping me up into a tight hug, Rux replied with that grin on his face widening to the point of looking like it was gonna split his face apart, "Say less, sweetheart."

The End

EPILOGUE

KAI

I'd completely underestimated how much shit I had or how much of it was completely necessary that it'd needed to make this move. Instead of hiring movers, I'd enlisted the help of family and friends to get all of my things settled into the condo in Lakeland. It'd been an arduous day of back and forth to the truck we'd rented to drive my things up from Belleville and we'd finished about an hour ago. Now it was the two of us in the condo as everyone else had gone back down to Belleville.

"I got you something," I said to Rux suddenly.

I got up from the couch to go into my bedroom to dig through the tote that I'd stored the gift in until we had a chance to settle down.

"You know Christmas is still a few days out, right?" Rux cracked as he opened up the small three by five inch box that I'd stored the gift in.

Opening the box, Rux was quiet initially until he read the words on the gift and he let out a sharp bark of laughter. A few weeks ago, *MoretoLife* had compiled a holiday gift guide on the site with different trinkets from Amazon linked. I just about lost my mind when I saw the inclusion of one of the items and knew I'd be making a purchase as soon as I saw it.

"You like it?" I asked, helpless against falling into giggles myself.

Inside of the box was the spare set of keys to the condo with a keychain attached that read "I love you for who you are but *that dick* sure is a bonus". Rux was insistent about not having a set of keys to the condo even though I told him that I was good with it. I think he thought I'd get freaked out by the level of access it would grant, but I was also someone who lived for convenience, so I wasn't too put out by him keeping the spare set in his possession. It was a point of contention as we went back and forth for weeks, but all of that came to an end with this simple gift.

"I love it," he said, leaning down to press a soft kiss against my mouth, "and I love you, too."

AFTERWORD

ABOUT THE AUTHOR

Nicole Falls is a contemporary Black romance writer who firmly believes in the power of Black love stories being told. She's also a ceramic mug and lapel pin enthusiast who cannot function without her wireless Beats constantly blaring music. When Nicole isn't writing, she spends her time singing off key to her Tidal and/or Spotify playlists while drinking coffee and/or cocktails! She currently resides in the suburbs of Chicago.

ALSO BY NICOLE FALLS

CPSIA information can be obtained
at www.ICGtesting.com
Printed in the USA
LVHW041528231219
641484LV00005B/1004/P